Praise for Kevin MacNeil

A Method Actor's Guide to Jekyll and Hyde

'Kevin MacNeil's new novel may well be the last, and funniest, word on Scotland's national schizophrenia'
STUART KELLY

'Cleverly constructed and entertaining'
DAILY MAIL

'A wonderful romp of a book ... a funny, irreverent and moving 21st-century look at human nature'
DOUG JOHNSTONE, THE HERALD

'Written with insight, wit and wisdom, it's a black comedy with serious things to say'
THE BIG ISSUE

'One of the most down-the-line enjoyable fiction reads of the year'
THE LIST, BEST BOOKS OF 2010

'A fascinating read: darkly comic and deeply reflective'
ANNE DONOVAN

'A love letter to Edinburgh . . . I loved it'
SCOTLAND ON SUNDAY

'It is brilliant, touching, funny and clever. It is also a sign that Kevin MacNeil is only just starting. Some of you out there can look forward to another 30 or 40 years of such quality and better. You are very lucky. We are lucky'
ROGER HUTCHINSON, WEST HIGHLAND FREE PRESS

'A blackly funny story . . . MacNeil is an experienced and gifted novelist, who uses Edinburgh for a setting as expertly as Ian Rankin or Alexander McCall Smith, though quite differently from both'
SYDNEY MORNING HERALD, PICK OF THE WEEK

To Myles

A METHOD ACTOR'S GUIDE TO

with

JEKYLL AND HYDE

~A~ NOVEL

admiration and

all best wishes,

KEVIN MacNEIL

Kevin x

Polygon

First published in 2010 by Polygon; this paperback edition
published in 2011 by Polygon, an imprint of Birlinn Ltd
Birlinn Ltd
West Newington House
10 Newington Road
Edinburgh
EH9 1QS

www.polygonbooks.co.uk

ISBN 978 1 84697 183 9
ebook ISBN 978 0 85790 016 6

British Library Cataloguing-in-Publication Data
A catalogue record for this book is available on request from the British Library.

Typeset by IDSUK (DataConnection) Ltd

Printed in Great Britain by
Clays Ltd, St Ives plc

for the you you are

the you you'd like to be

the you you think you are

and the you, you, you, you

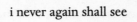

i never again shall see

'Everything is true...'
Robert

'Everything is true; only the opposite is true. . .'
Robert Louis

'Everything is true; only the opposite is true, too; you must believe both equally or be damned.'

Robert Louis Stevenson

PART ONE

The Unbearable Likeness of Being

I'm in two minds. I peer through the indifferent window and scrutinise the smudgy, almost picturesque Edinburgh skyline. I overlook my reflection, it makes me feel less self-conscious but more self-aware. The brightish grey midday sky could go either way. Why not err on the side of optimism? That holiday must have changed my outlook. I'm seeing blue skies where there aren't any. Funny thing about holidays, the skies seem to get brighter, the world more tolerable.

Decision made, I put aside the thin waterproof jacket and toss my cycling helmet on to the couch, opt instead for a white and black sweatshirt and that cool black and white beanie hat I got in Rome. Touch of Rome equals touch of style. The old fave shoes, though, the soft-soled cleated ones that clip into the pedals but don't make you walk like you have two planks glued to your shoes.

I feel wonderful today, got that devilish streak of omniscience about me. I can do anything.

Must've been the change of scenery. Oh, I can make a joke about that at rehearsals. Change of scenery. They probably still don't have the scenery and props ready. Well, to quote my tattoo, 'Lift your bike out into the open day. Ride forth.'

If my current state of mind had a tattoo it would read, 'Come at me, world, I'm ready for you.'

I clip the shoes into the pedals of my single-speed fixed-gear bike and set off into the growling traffic. No changeable gears.

How can you cycle around Edinburgh (built, like Rome, on seven hills) when you have no gears? I have surplus. All my gears are in my legs, like all my characters are in my mind. I contain multitudes.

A mild fog begins to descend and I realise I've left my lights at home. I must've been using them on the road-bike – my superfast racing bike – before I left for Rome. I pump my legs up and down on the pedals, trying to find my rhythm, or as cyclists call it, *cadence*, all the while deep-breathing the typical old reek that I love and hate – greenness and exhaust fumes and breweries. The first few dozen turns of the legs, up the street – dodging negligent cars and lemming-wannabe pedestrians – are always weirdly tough and just when your heart and legs and mind find rhythm, the first traffic lights sail towards you. Red. Every time.

Today I'm unclipping my left shoe in anticipation of red when I realise the lights are green. Green like hope. A good omen. I reclip and shoot on, legs working hard, through the junction. Somebody over there beeps their horn swift as urgency, but that's the impertinence of drivers for you. I'm the one who's saving the planet, mate. I'm the one with the tree-trunk thighs. I'm the one with the resting pulse of 40, the enormous heart. So go learn what you're doing to the planet. Kids, or *their* kids, will probably grow up to build time machines *just* to come back and torture us for wasting their world. Serve us right.

I'm feeling immortal, so it's all good.

I hope I can still remember my lines. Mind you, Mac – the playwright – is only going to keep changing them anyway. Don't know whether I like him or hate him. There's something wrong with him. Bloody writers. Their heads aren't screwed on right.

I haven't seen the others since we had to take a semi-welcome break due to financial complications. The production was running out of cash; a funding application they'd been depending on 'tragically achieved but half its financial ambition'. Paul 'the Jewel' Blinkbonny, our pathetic semi-flamboyant director, wept a few tears and almost realistic they were, too.

I didn't think about my fellow actors all that much in Rome. Except Juliette. I should have asked her to come with me. Leaving without telling anyone except her felt rebellious and Bohemian. Sometimes you need a change, you just can't help yourself.

As I'm cycling the five miles to Theatre Lothian in the city centre, I lose myself to The Flow, the poetic motion of traffic all in accordance with itself, like destiny made manifest. We're all moving together, and it makes us feel like we belong together in this now, this *us*. Yep, I'm fizzing inside with an easy adrenaline. I can do *anything*. It's going to be a good day. I'll remember my lines. I had some ideas and maybe Mac'll take some of my suggestions and run with them. He can run as far as he likes, long as he doesn't come back. Ha ha. I might give him that one, if only to see him crack half a smile. No, he wouldn't laugh. I don't think I do like him.

Edinburgh. Even when she's ugly she's beautiful. Riding here, I reflect mindlessly on how this city's a dizzy amalgam of bored self-hating graffiti-splattered council houses and self-important bespoke-logo'd administrative hubs. I cycle on and the air itself buoys me along. I belong to the air and light, not the ridiculous fake world of commerce and routine and real jobs and lower and upper-class thugs. I am a free spirit, I am an artiste and I am invincible.

I keep my breathing regular, I let my legs push the never-ending gorgeous grotesque city behind me, that hotbed of genius and sleaze. Auld Reekie. Dùn Èideann.

I'm so at one with things I could probably close my eyes and get to Theatre Lothian just as easily. I ride along pedalling and breathing pedalling and breathing pedalling and breathing and ideas ride along within me at their own cadence, on their own thoughtwaves . . . The phrase 'Living in Edinburgh' comes randomly to mind. I wonder about life, what it means to be alive. I wonder about Edinburgh, this physical construct that becomes a spiritual part of you. I wonder about how I came to be here, in this life, where I am part of Edinburgh though it is bigger than me and I am bigger than it.

After drama college – and all the real-life drama that led up to it – I decided Edinburgh would be a wicked place to settle. Fair foul city-sized village of bustling summers and introspective autumns, backdrop to the world's largest arts festival and all its anticipated serendipities. Home to a national parish council, an almost powerful parliament indolently bustling with her irrec-oncilable flow of accurate rumours and unreliable press releases. Provocative, conservative Auld Reekie. The tiny capital of our proud-to-be-humble and fighting-to-be-fought-for nation that isn't a nation, where our new Old Testament God has cursed us with a fear of failure and blessed us with a fear of success. Where Highlander and Lowlander alike can agree to disagree on this and that because everything is contradiction and it is precariousness itself that holds things together.

Edinburgh.

An awful good place to be an actor.

Since I spend most of my time learning lines, or writing lines – I have pretentions in that area, too – I'm often alone. Even though I am beginning to despise writers, I went through a phase in my early teens when I wanted to write a book about loveliness. Yes, the world's very loveliness. But the world sooner rather than later is a sour-hearted place. The rapes and childbeatings and bullyings and murders and human traffickings and innumerable injustices you read about every day are not lovely, they're inescapably real.

As I cycle, memories from real life pass me like cars. There goes a scruffy old Reliant Robin sputtering along, trundling towards a slow corner, putting me in mind of my agent, Dickie Clovenstone.

With the bad comes the good; I always manage to win through. I've been awarded the lead role – that is, lead role*s* – in a new stage version of *The Strange Case of Dr Jekyll and Mr Hyde*. Even Dickie – that two-faced old failed playboy, arthritic, asthmatic and alcoholic – couldn't conceal his shock.

'Well, boy, I'm delighted! Oh, I'm thrilled to bits!' He moved through his fug of cigarette smoke towards me, arms crucified. His eyes, normally dead in their spectacles like damaged headlights, registered real shock and pseudo-delight. An actor can always read another person's eyes. He wrapped me in an own-brand-whisky-and-Old-Spice-soaked hug that made me flinch for buried reasons. 'First big job – and it's a belter!'

Well, it is and it isn't. I want – I need – to be famous. Wealthy. Admired. Hell, *loved*.

Jekyll & Hyde, as Mac has presumptuously called it, is really quite a low-budget play, but, hey, it might be good. A few more weeks of rehearsal in Edinburgh then off on tour: Edinburgh, Glasgow, Aberdeen, Stornoway, Brighton, London. As long as I get a fee and something *actual* to put on my CV I don't care how big or small their budget is. The important fact is, they *want* me. It feels right – to be needed, I mean.

The audition was easy for the chancer I am. Truth is, I went to dozens of schools but I never had much schooling. I left my final secondary school with a pass in English, an unwarranted smirk and a pocketful of borrowed money.

7

A beige Volkswagen Jetta drifts past at I'd guess a steady 29 mph. It has a bumper sticker that says 'A Good Bumper Sticker Makes Me Feel Like I'm Done Thinking for the Day'. Reminds me of The Shrivel.

When I left school, I had real dreams, though cynicism and distrust are common in foster children, according to The Shrivel (my name for my shrink). He also told me that a quarter of foster children are homeless within a year of leaving home.

'Well,' I said, 'I've been homeless *all my life*. How could I leave home when I never had one?'

He gave a patronising cough. 'Now, don't, don't exaggerate. You had, you had . . . seventeen homes.' He did an involuntary double-take which made me splutter with laughter. '*Seventeen*?'

'That's what I said. I never had *one*.'

'I'm not, I'm not sure you understand the seriousness of the –'

'No, man. It's you that doesn't see it. I'm gonna be famous. I'm the guy that's gonna redefine what famous even *means*.'

For maybe half a minute The Shrivel gazed at me without speaking. At last his eyes blinked and they seemed to say, *I believe you, almost.*

'Well, it's, it's good to have ambition,' he conceded.

I must send him a flyer. *Jekyll & Hyde* – the old bastard'll be overjoyed for me. Give himself credit for it too, no doubt, but that's okay, no biggie. He only meant well, when he meant anything.

Out the corner of my eye, something shadowy as a bat's wing startles me. A BMW rocketing past. Its stupid black polished length flits fast over my reflection, like it's trying to smack my elbow. Yeah, that's okay, if you hit me it would only be me who got killed and you who got away with it. Tosser. Like something Whitekirk would drive.

My college days also played out in Edinburgh. To get into college, I wallpapered the truth. Well, I lied like my life depended on it. How else does someone like me get to do Acting and Performance thankyouverymuch?

Whitekirk, the college Head of Drama, soon discovered I had lied. An ominously neutral letter summoned me to his office. Godfrey Whitekirk was an overweight headmasterish fiftysomething with milky hair that reminded me of a Mr Whippy ice-cream. He sat rigid behind an oak desk, his face turning crimson, his eyes burning malevolence at me. You didn't need to be an actor to read the curses in those eyes.

Impassive, I held his gaze.

The long silence he extended was supposed to unnerve me (hadn't he himself taught that particular class?) Somewhere outside, a bird gave a sweet chirrupy chortle. A twinge of joy in the ecstasy of this drama, this real-life tension with unwritten repercussions. I felt wild with hidden confidence.

'Sit. Down.'

'Yes, sir. Thank you, sir.' I kept my face blank.

'*You.*' He shook his head. '*You. Lied. To. Me.*' His breathing was laboured. Heart attack within a decade, I'd say.

'Sir?' Sir, being quite rare nowadays, is a more marvellous ingratiator than ever. I widened my eyes in respect. Play it right.

'*Your qualifications.*'

'Ah . . .' I slumped, blinked back an imaginary tear. I took a deep breath, bent back a fingernail till it hurt bad, swallowed the wince and wept a few pained tears. 'This day . . . this day had to come . . .'

'Did you *really* think you'd get away with it? Didn't you think we'd have a system in place to, to *root out this sort of thing*? Heavens, boy, don't you think every Tom, Dick and Debbie Harry would be in college if it was that easy?'

I kept a straight face. He was famous among students for remixing the cliché. 'Sir, no, sir.'

'And to think *I believed you*. I interviewed you right here in this office. This is serious, very serious. What you've done is actually *illegal* . . . Do you have anything to say for yourself?'

'Sir . . .' Measure the pause. Deflate body further, cast eyes to the floor. Blink. Blink back meek tears. 'No, sir.'

'*No?*'

I glanced up, puppy-eyed. His face bulged, a talking pumpkin. He gripped the desk, on the verge of getting to his feet.

Keep cool. This is working.

Now speak in a quiet, honest manner. 'Well, sir, you see, I was desperate – *desperate* – to get into drama school. *This* school. I told you I was adopted and had a tough upbringing – I mean, *really* tough. Uh, and when I said that my house burned down and my exam certificate was incinerated and that the Scottish Qualification Authority . . . Sir?'

'*You're nothing but a liar!*'

I wondered if a blood vessel might burst and spread a little red inkstain over the white of his eye.

I conceded, 'There, uh, there *was* no fire.'

'*You sat there –? You sat there and sold me a grizzly bear-faced packet of lies?* Even – even said *that your parents had died in that fire*. Oh, I had thought twice about calling the police, but not now.' He picked up the phone receiver with his left hand and with his other stabbed a fat finger at the key pad. 'I'll have your nuts for garters, boy.'

'Well –'

'Well what? Oh, there's no talking me round! You sat – you *cried* in my office! *You . . . deceitful . . . little . . . toe-rug.*'

'Well, you're right, sir, I did cry.' (I had actually bent my entire ring-fingernail right back, every bit as excruciating as it

10

sounds.) 'I told you about the fire in every detail. About my birth parents – my mother's tough love, my father's belief that a child should only eat what it has seen in cartoon form in an advert on telly, I told you about how important drama was in my life and how playing *Hamlet* in a school production literally saved my life.'

Whitekirk gave a grunt-and-nod. The phone receiver hovered in his hand.

'And I also told you about how my kitten – remember fluffy wee Rosencrantz? – perished in the fire. How my parents were too – ah, *dismissive* – of the arts to come and see me that night, the highlight of my life, portraying *Hamlet*. And how when my mother's discarded and, and *drunken* cigarette torched the place that night and –'

'Yes?'

'Sir, you – if I may be so bold – more or less shed a tear with me that day.'

Silence.

'Sir, *I convinced you.*'

The silence deepened and shifted.

'Sir, *I'm. A good. Actor.*' I sent a fierce pleading blazing through my eyes.

Oh, damn it, I was good.

In slow motion, the phone receiver returned to its cradle.

'Sir, I have a talent. I beg of you to let me develop it. If I can act well enough to persuade you – *you, sir* – does that not make me worthy of a place on this course?'

Ha!

I grin to think about it now, hurtling through the Edinburgh traffic, swinging out past a 26 bus that's painted zebra style for somebody-craving-money reasons. Odd world. I up my tempo; the mist can't harm The Flow.

11

Not everything at college was quite so easy. During my three years I had to work about 200 per cent harder than the others; Whitekirk had instructed the lecturers to keep a suspicious eye trained on me. I knew that if I stepped out of line – or, rather, if I got caught – I'd be kicked off the course faster than you could say Konstantin Sergejevitch Stanislavski.

Some classes were useful, most were pretentious. The warm-up exercises for body and voice were a weird torture. They should have just made us all go out for a bike ride, shouting at occasional motorists.

I boost my cadence again as nostalgia's adrenaline revs within me. The wet mist is a cold sweat. Cleansing, though, in its own way. Odd, how things are, when you really look at them, also what they're not.

At the beginning we studied in playful earnest. Voice and speech, singing, body awareness, phonetics, dance, stage combat, improv, textual analysis and so on.

Under my beanie hat, lecturers' voices rise above the rumbling and gurning of traffic.

'To play a drunk, one must be as a drunk trying to act sober.'

'To die well one must struggle for life.'

'Fully to be something is to embrace its opposite.'

'Not acting but reacting.'

'Not reacting but being.'

'Aye being where extremes meet.'

Most of the students hid their insecurities behind masks of arrogance, self-centredness and vanity; I didn't much like that, as I was doing the same thing myself. Pub culture was a bit embarrassing as alcohol tended to increase my fellow students' me-me-me-ness, their potential for histrionics, their (already clamorous) volume level.

Everyone can't be the most important person in the room.

These attitudes lead to outrageous drunken behaviours which could only be tolerated in certain pubs and given that *we* often felt we'd had too much of ourselves, it's no wonder we never felt welcome enough in one place to make it our regular. Acting students. We weren't friends, we were people bonded together by other people's masks, other people's lies.

Some students who, as I did, stayed in halls of residence, invented a game they called 'Roommate Roulette', which was a kind of 'Spin the Bottle' with roomkeys, nightclub flyers and condoms. You could end up with someone you didn't get along with, maybe someone of the same sex; no one seemed to mind. After all, these were zany (read: vain) drama students who were living out colourful scenes for their future biographers. I spray-painted *Self-Mythologisers 'R' Us* on a bedsheet and hung it from the railings outside one particularly hedonistic student house. But it was all in the name of art. The delicate art of *bullshit-and-we-know-it*.

Not that I'm one – not that I'm one to talk. There was this night I figured the hell with it and took a blind leap off the teetotal wagon and into some dark, peat-reeking whisky ditch. No one ever mentioned to me the alcoholic night, the night that thirsted for something *different*, the night that drank itself stupid on its own oblivion and spent the following day on its knees spewing steadily darkening bile into the toilet. It was unsettling and weird to survive a night that only existed in an image or two.

Like those girls in, *Burke and Hare*, was it? Half-undressed in flash clothes. Performing bored gyrations on the dance floor, their bodies strobed by a bombed rainbow of disco lights. Their honed innocence said *Look at me* and my feigned worldliness replied *I won't look at you closely, for you are frost in the heart and fire in the blood. I don't give in to temptations like that. I control my emotions. I am an ac-tor.* Then blackness and the feeling that something had happened . . .

The toilet – not pristine – squatted there the following day, silently affirming reality and hinting at guilts. I thought I'd been in a fight with someone. There was a girl, a guy . . . A torrent of shame in my stomach erupted and burst its acid way through my mouth in a fierce lumpy jet.

The night that didn't exist and the day that reeked of death are both gone now, perhaps secreted in some part of the judgemental mind. Sooner or later I decided that the world had moved on and I should too. I vowed never to drink again, satisfied all the same that if I had done or said something wrong good-and-proper I'd have heard of it by now. And I stuck to my vow, more or less.

Yes, no, college – see, I was breaking off from the main group. I didn't like drink for what it had done to me, but I enjoyed pub culture, I liked the atmosphere that groups of near-random people create when officially relaxing.

Up London Road now, moving faster, cars and buses and taxis and lorries whooshing and honking with impatience. On a bike you're both tortoise and hare as the moment demands. I swerve between two 'Chelsea tractors', my right shoulder clipping the wing mirror of one; it beeps at me twice, but I flash the guy a manual insult then shrug the incident off. My inner life is more interesting. Memories are reanimating my mind. This mist is awesome, like the city is flooding with dry ice.

A huge multicoloured dairy truck barges past, noisy, swift, emboldened by its own momentum.

One of our more flamboyant lecturers, Fenella Prestonpans, dress size 22 if she was a day, used to differentiate between us 'artistes' and 'mice'. I can still picture her as she earthquaked into the room, resplendent in a cake-splattered tent, hairy green tights and improbable red ballet shoes, like Dorothy gone wrong. 'All right, everyone, find a space,' she'd bellow. 'And listen the bloody heck up. There are those who live their lives not under the spotlight but under little selfish private reading lights or in front of the garish pig-ignorant light of a TV screen. To some extent these are the ordinaries, the nonentities. They are mice. They have sweet flip all *character*. They are the masses. But without them, you would not have an acting career – as I hope some of you will. *You are not the mice.* You are the public people. The stars. The *heroes*, if you will. The *loud* people. The *characters*. Bright – brash – noisy – colourful – unapologetic. So. Listen.

'You. Must live. Your lives. In a very. Big. Way.'

This idea appealed to me. Ambition firestormed my mind. I was mad with freedom. So I had a demented brainwave. I turned my life into a series of scenes and plays.

I took to going to pubs *in character*. Thus, I could have fun *and* hone my acting skills at the same time. In my own mind I was making myself The One Most Likely to Become Famous.

I would liberate clothing, temporary hair dyes, wigs and props from the 'locked' Costume & Scenery department and spend a weekend learning as much from 'real' life as I'd learned during the past month's 'how to be fake' classes. A besuited version of me – 'Olly', Eton old-boy, dealer in the City, Porsche Cayman S and homes in Edinburgh, London and New York – would shark the classier wine bars, mooching drinks off slim sleek-haired businesswomen who had moneyed a decade or so off their age. Five o'clock on Friday would see 'Jimmy the joiner' dumping his toolbag (actually filled with cutlery) in a grimy no-frills bar off Leith Walk, relaxing with a contented sigh into his thirsty drink, cursing his team's misfortunes. Camper than a jamboree, 'Leslie Love' would flounce into Each Way Bette's demanding 'something long and hard, sweetie, and get me a drink while you're at it'. I went to student unions as a Goth, an emo, a raver, a 'new lad'. Must've met hundreds of people I never saw again – or rather, they never saw 'me' again. Hundreds. And I learned so damn *much*.

I assimilated all the tricks. Stolen car-brand keyrings, aftershave samples from chemists, coloured contact lenses, accessorisation, the diverse wonders of hairstyling. And above all – using one's eyes. That's what they're for. Eyes are an actor's greatest asset.

I became in all things a free actor in the world.

But even I could see that things were rotten in the land of tasty pastries and Hans Christian. An old niggle was resurfacing . . .

My legs arced the bike and I flew past a zigzagging fat man on a mountain bike. I skimmed him close enough to give him a valuable-lesson wobble.

I brought it up with The Shrivel, how difficult it was to be myself. I'd been coming to his clinically lit 'Beige Furniture and Regulation Big Green Plant'-style office in the New Town – the posh part of Edinburgh – for some time now. It was via the NHS, but true to my make-believe nature, I'd blagged myself a private psychiatrist with a public reputation. The Shrivel was a curious man, although quite beige himself in some ways. His favourite infuriating habit was scribbling notes – dividing his attention – at random times during our appointments. Worse, he could even do this while *he* was talking. I got over my annoyance by pretending he was drawing sketches of Freud taking him and his mother to bed. He wore a precise goatee beard which looked fake and annoying tiny rectangular glasses that he would drive into his forehead when he wasn't scratching at his notebook. He was overweight, sweaty and restless.

Our first meeting was less than auspicious. A large white desk-fan circled upon itself, sluggish with boredom. 'You've had a . . . challenging upbringing. Most people could . . . could hardly imagine how that would make a person feel about themselves. Hmm?' His voice was gentle and artificial the way a little girl's is when she's talking to her dolls.

'You know, I feel like that mental patient whose shrivel, I mean shrink – psychiatrist – fell into a deep pond at the hospital and started drowning. So the patient jumped in and saved the doctor's life.'

Pause here for effect, and to register his professionally controlled confusion. His eyes said, *Has he finished? What does he mean?*

After a while, I resumed. 'And so they said to the patient, "There's good news and bad. You saved your doctor's life, and for that we recognise you have come to learn the difference between right and wrong. In fact, we're going to release you.

"But you'll be sad to hear that the doctor probably went into the pond deliberately, because he was later found in the bathroom with a noose around his neck.

"Hell no," says the patient. "I left him hanging there to dry."'

The Shrivel looked hurt – he blanched – and I retracted more or less straightaway. 'Hey, no, no, man – I was kidding. Kidding. Sense of humour, man. It's all good. Just testing the water. Seems *icy*. Chill, Sigmund.'

The rest of that appointment zipped past in a bland blur. He asked me questions, I adopted a persona a couple or three removes from myself and gave polite, stilted answers. His tiny rectangular specs could see he wasn't getting anywhere with me. Scribble scribble. 'Okay. Early days. It would make me happy if, if you could find some time to fill out this short form for me for next time, all right? Is that, is that okay, hmm? What I think, I think is, even this early on, is, is, and it's likely, something has, has consolidated your own sense of defensiveness, of life itself as, as shadowy, haunted by, by forces of, of, well, not evil, but sinister, hmm . . .?'

The buggering hell was he on about? Filling in the form was easy enough. I didn't know a lot of the factual information – for the question 'How would you describe your upbringing?' I just wrote 'Upbringing *singular?*' and likewise 'How would you describe your relationship with your parents?' 'Which ones?'

This part was easier: 'List the things you like.'

Fame, stage and screen stuff, drama, cycling, wild animals, reading and watching and maybe writing plays, walking, freedom, containing multitudes, falling asleep but only when I'm very tired otherwise I loathe it, the Scottish sense of humour, the cool sad song of the wood pigeon, doing stuff that's a bit offbeat, listening to the radio very late at night/very early in the morning, black, white, hearing a really good joke for the first time, random acts of art, the electric guitar, the acoustic guitar, Christian aliens riding dinosaurs bareback.

'List the things you don't like.'

Grrr. Mushrooms (evil! evil! – the spawn of Satan), violence, violent peace activists, arrogance, false modesty, answering the phone, drivers who don't think cyclists exist, death, not knowing if you know that person well enough to say hello far less speak to them, guilt, hearing my own heartbeat, injustice, people who are too controlling, blandness, people who tell lies. Filling in forms. Hypocrisy. People who doodle sketches of themselves going to bed with Freud's mother.

I was surprised that the list of things I don't like was shorter than the list of things I do. That wasn't true to character. But who among us is?

The reason I wanted to be an actor – not so much according to The Shrivel as according to what I told The Shrivel – was I had no fixed identity. And if I couldn't be myself, I'd have to be somebody else. Anybody. Everybody.

18

Thus, drama college didn't so much make the man I am today as the men I'm not.

I come to, cycling along. The mist is dispersing. Weird, how the hypnotic rhythms of bike-riding lull you into such a state of relaxation you can cycle a mile or two and you can't even remember doing it. The steady rhythms of your feet on the pedals and the pedals on the chainring and the chainring on the chain and the chain on the sprocket and the sprocket on the hub and the hub on the wheel and the wheels on the street, the street that buzzes with other wheels will lull will lull will lull you into a daydream. I smile to myself. The Flow always looks after you. You and The Flow are one, not two. *I lose myself* in cycling. I don't know why that should be such a good thing, but it is. Physical exercise makes a tangible difference to the heart's properties.

The mist's all but lifted now – already – strange; it has shrunk away to near-nothing, like breath on a windowpane. Cars, buses, taxis, lorries – the traffic has duplicated itself a few times over, now we're nearer the stone and glass heart of the city.

I pedal faster because I can see further and because my pumped-up heart muscle and the fluidity of the moment and the visual and tactile grace of my bike demand it. I wonder if I look as confident and as part-of-the-moment as I feel. I pity pedestrians, who have to go about the day heavy and slow. I'm at my most alive when riding The Flow or when I'm being someone else under the lights, before the audience. That's the funny thing about life –

Blackness.

?

Swifter than shock: aggressive blackness. A screech of dark-walloping-metallic-flying-twisting-concrete blackness. A groan. Mine.

Broken.

Wrong.

Floaty, no body.

Dead?

To die well one must struggle for life.

But.

Urrggghhhhhhhhhhhhhhhhhhh.

Well, Godbastarddamnit.

Fading.

Noise.

Okay.

Take it in.

I open my eyes. *Try* to. Traffic sounds rumble like the sea in some inner distance. Also there is a jabby kind of blaring, an insistent something, like a parent. Someone else's. A shuddering inside. I wish everything would leave me alone. So tired.

Why can't my eyes ope– ah. Hang on. That's it, raise the curtain. My mind throbs with dull noises and distorted light. I weigh nothing. Channels of noise and light are passing through me. I can't link them with anything. I dimly wonder if I'm still me or if the blackness has broken my head too much. Where is my head? I am numb. I know enough to know this is some kind of Upheaval, one way or the other.

I wonder if I'm fine or if I'm damaged for ever. I wonder if I'm going to die. And at the same time – like a burst of pain – *already? No!* There is a play, is there not? And there is fame and money. The world cannot change me. The world cannot change me like this. The world cannot change me like this before I have changed *it*.

My skull hurts.

This is good, maybe.

Up there, above my left eye.

A pain that is big *and* sharp at once. How would you picture that? Like a cloud with a rocketship inside it. A mist with a swift bike.

Wait – good? How?

Pain means I am alive. Because one thing you can say about pain, pain is a proof of life. Yes, a little pain never hurt anyone. The noises and lights and images are moving and I'll need to sort them out, but I know I'm still a part of – of that which has *no* resting place.

The dizzying light slows a little. I can't see much. White, is all. A big ugly circle – wait, that's a man's head. Face. A bald face with. No, a bald head and a face with a moustache. Well, the rest of the stuff must be sky. Hello, sky. Thank you. Sort of. Hang on.

Almost before I think it, I decide that if I'm alive and have a body I'm ready to move. I try to sit, I push forward – my mind spins like a sick fairground – someone's hand is at my back (good, I have, I mean, I can feel a back, my back), their hand supports me, the bald man's hand I think helps me to a nearly sitting position.

Oooh. This is not the way to be alive. Everything spins.

The disjointed feeling of *blood*. A part of me that should be inside me is outside of me. I feel funny. Dizzy and weak, like joy. No, not joy. I bring my left hand from nowhere up to my head. Interesting, I have a left arm. My left arm works. Blood. It is good to find bits that are working. The blood from a big

21

throb-throb-throb gash in my forehead trickles warm then cold down the side of my face. What day is it today? Ah, the blood is warm, my face is cold. I goosebump. I want to be hugged up in a huge blanket. Where's my mammy? Oh, I never had one. Did I? The blood that's still inside my veins tingles in dazed excitement. Oh boy, normally I can do things much better than this. What's my name, though? Wait, is someone else asking me that? Who said what day is it?

My head sways, lolls a circle or two. The world is wrong, puke-y, too fast.

Breathing is bad. No, breathing is good. My breathing is bad. Blood outside is bad. Um – having movement is good. Or bad? Being able to move must be good, like how I'd forgotten I had a left arm till I moved it. What other bits do I have? Maybe they will all come alive when I remember them and move them.

A small crowd has gathered round. Some of them closer than others. Some of them talking as if nothing has happened. They should get the hell away.

Where's my blanket?

I don't have a blanket. I was a foster child.

I do and don't want people looking at me. I like it when people look at me. But I'm not me. I'm better than this. Cleverer.

Must look stupid sitting here. Oh, I could die of embarrass – no, wait. Shut up. Don't know my own name. I *am* stupid. Try to make things make sense. Make sense of things. Right. That noise, say, coming from near the pavement, that is words, that is a man making words. No moustache. A man in a green costume. Dark hair. I think he's asking me my name. I can't tell him what I don't know.

On the other side, Bald Moustache is looking at me like I am a ghost. Stupid man. I'm not a ghost, I'm a stupid man.

Another noise. 'Uh-w-wh-wh–.' Ooh, that's exciting – that sound came from me. Ah, yes, I know: I'm trying to ask if my bike is okay.

All that is coming out of me is blood and nonsense.

And the green man has become two green men. They are apologising to me, I don't know why. Now they are moving me, which means I am getting fixed. They're lifting me. How can they do that? Oh, yeah, I don't weigh anything. My head spins like the wheel of a bike when it isn't broken. My head therefore is not broken.

Take me away, green men, I hope you will drive safely. I hope you will fix my bike. You better have my bike somewhere in this fancy UFO van, flashing with lights, you are putting me into, upside down on my back. I think – yes – my bike is green. You will like it. It will match you. Make sure the wheels are round.

Goodbye everyone gathered here who isn't green, thanks for coming to the show.

Sorry I couldn't remember my own name.

A regular high-pitched *beep* . . . *beep* punctuates the thick anti-septic air. Pain. *Bad* pain. Every nerve end shrill with pain. My whole body is a fingernail bent back. Can't live like –

Ah, what's that? That feels good. Happy numbness swimming in my veins.

Imagine.

Ah, weird bliss.

What if I just went out into the world as myself and sat at a table outside a pleasant café with a cappuccino in front of me and a pair of sunglasses flattering my eyes and a book draped across my lap and a relaxed and welcoming expression on my face?

And what if I watched and waited. Watched the cobbled street particular to this part of the universe, the girls swaying past, their smiles highlighting unknown conversations and the muted sun glinting off tabletops and shop windows in a warm humble sparkle. *Life*.

And what if I waited for a girl to come along, and a girl came along and she pointed a glistening finger at a chair and said, 'D'you mind if I –?'

I'd make my face and voice suave and say, 'Be my guest.'

And already I would have lost because in giving my face a sophisticated expression and my voice some kind of urbane timbre, I would have stopped being myself.

Then, wow.

That first time the *Jekyll & Hyde* cast came together was the first time I set eyes on her, and my idea of loveliness was born anew. Juliette was like Edinburgh, a palpable mirage. And she was so nice to me. It felt amazing for someone so beautiful to treat me like a person worthy of her attention, much less an equal. Also present, though less so, were my fellow cast members, the director, the stage manager.

Juliette and I had to act a scene from a play as a warm-up exercise.

But a scene from a different play, a play of the imagination, a hallu-cination, came to life in my mind as I looked at this elegant young woman. *I fantasised that I was thrust – by destiny – into a situation where I and only I could save her life. She was crossing the street – it was London Road – and she had white earphones in her cute ears and she was listening to her music with such raptness that she paid no attention to the traffic. I believed that she could rest assured the traffic itself would pay sufficient attention to her, that she never needed to look before she crossed the road. She was not one of the normal people, the lemmings, because the world took too much notice of her. A large maroon brute of a bus, however, was careering down the road, headed straight for her, too fast, she hadn't seen it, she was nodding almost imperceptible acknowledgement to her music, a light smile playing on her lips, and the bus raced towards her and just when it was almost upon her I launched myself out into the middle of the road and grabbed hold of her petite frame and my cyclist's thighs vaulted us both out of harm's way. The bus shot past, clipping my shoulder as it did, but I didn't flinch. She removed her earphones and looked into my eyes with awe.*

Now she owed me her life . . .

In the rehearsal room, we were to improvise a scene from a play, in order to get to know each other because that useless writer – Mac, wasn't he there as well? – forgot the script or more likely hadn't written it yet, and the scene we were doing, Juliette and I, it was . . . We were playing – yes, I was a Glaswegian junkie on a hotel corridor floor and she was an East European chambermaid. I was suffering. I was fevered and shivering and she wanted to hold me, to comfort me. At the same time I repelled her. My body was rank, I was falling apart.

My heart was racing, some of my juddering was real because my heart was thumping so hard against my chest it made my skinny arms pulsate. I made myself look pitiful. I was hideous. Juliette recoiled. She couldn't help me. She couldn't speak English. (Juliette spoke an invented spontaneous language that sounded kind of East European.) She couldn't bring herself to touch me. I needed her to touch me. We both had the idea I was dying.

Great effort, great acting, some of which wasn't acting. You can't control the heart like that. I managed a single massive syllable through my parched and dying lips, 'Hug.'

And she, resolved now to helping me, no matter how repugnant I was, thought I needed something from my backpack, which lay invisibly beside me. She grappled around in it, and withdrew from that bag, her eyes alight with fear and wonder, a needle and she looked into my eyes soft and earnest and I looked into her eyes long and hard and the answer was

was that she pulled up my sleeve, pressed at a vein in my skinny arm and plunged that needle into me

like a nurse with a short sharp cure

and ooooh that feels good, warmth, every person who wants a hug knows that a true hug is impossible, you're trying to bring that person's warmth inside you, and this drug, it was hugging me from the inside, it was holding me inside, holding me together, it helped to make me me . . .

The Jekyll & Hyde was a hokey themed bar on the almost well-named Hanover Street. It was decorated throughout with a Gothic theme, the best part being the toilet doors; they were almost invisible, hidden brilliantly, bafflingly, in a wall that looked like a bookcase.

I nodded at them. 'Novel.'

After a few cocktails in the delightful gloom, she loosened up a little. I was drinking Red Bull, the hardest soft drink. Her loosening up loosened me up. I hoped she'd have a few more drinks, get properly drunk, but at ten-thirty she reached for her coat and, though I made sure she could see I was crestfallen, she insisted she had to get home early so she'd be fresh for rehearsals tomorrow.

Outside, a dense mist gave the pub's real flame lamps a syrupy, almost mawkish quality. As we walked, cars swished past slowly in the mist and in the romantic atmosphere other couples emerged and vanished. In the pearly dimness between two streetlamps we came to a mutual halt and stood facing each other. Old Edinburgh streetlamps are, as RLS once said, as lovely as the stars themselves; they still are, even in their sodium glow, beautiful, like the visible ghosts of longdead stars we see on big meaningful nights like this, nights that are dying as they happen.

I leaned in to kiss her and at the last moment she turned her face away from mine, like someone had called her name.

No one had.

'Why did you do that?' she asked.

I took a stunned moment to answer. 'I was just about to ask you the same thing.'

'I . . . It's never a good idea to get involved with artists in the same production.'

We both said 'sorry' at the same time.

She looked down for a while and took my hand in hers. I couldn't tell if her hand was entirely Platonic. We began walking again, strolling towards Princes Street. Her hand was soft and warm, and soon we both knew that our holding hands like this did have meaning. We shared our thoughts. We shared our solitudes. We *knew* we were sooner or later going to be together. We walked about the city centre for another hour or so, seldom speaking, and at one and the same time we both realised, hey, the mist's lifted, when did that happen?

At Juliette's suggestion, we took that usually arduous and tonight effortless walk up to the top of Calton Hill, the lovely place that is partly lovely because of its much lovelier view. Like a woman you love, but more, so much more – she loves you back.

Glittering beneath us lay Edinburgh and the Firth of Forth and the near-distant non-kingdom Kingdom of Fife. Over there was the castle, exquisite and menacing. Across there, the dead, haunting volcano of Arthur's Seat. Southside, the Old Town bristled with beautiful spires and random tenement rooftops, cramped closes and wide swift roads. An area of naive student geniuses and wisdom-belching pub bores. Northside presented one with the New Town, where the architecture grew autocratic and the Georgian dwellings held themselves with regimental self-regard, like minor royalty on longstanding parade.

Juliette and I held hands and savoured the view. She lay her head on my shoulders and snuggled in as the wind grew nippy. I turned her towards me and pulled her tight, held her close, as close as an eye, as close as a corneal graft, so close it became hard to tell which part of us was me, and which part her. Being an us was so fulfilling I realised letting go of her – as at one point I must – would be like a tearing apart, except that the pain – and it would be actual pain – was not physical but emotional.

At length I said, 'Can we go down there to Waverley?'

'As in railway station? Why?'

'I love the drama of railway stations. All those people leaving or coming together. The lovers and families meeting and parting and – just – peoplewatching. It's the actor in me.'

'Okay.'

She retrieved her hand from mine and I felt a stabbing panic in my chest. I grabbed back on to her hand. 'So you don't slip.'

All was well. Some things are too beautiful to lose.

As we walked hand in hand down the steps to the station I had a vertiginous feeling like I could happily fall headlong down the concrete steps in a mad tumbling love with this beautiful woman who made me feel like someone else, like someone . . . better.

And who had already said no.

Hmm.

Halfway down I halted and turned her towards me in the soft half-light.

'I really like you. What can I do about that?'

She smiled. 'If I told you I'm really not a nice person once you get to know me properly, would you believe me?'

'No.'

'I can be a real bitch.'

'Impossible.'

'No, really. I'm not as sweet and innocent as you seem to think.'

'I don't care if you have flaws; you're perfect.'

'Do you always idealise people?'

'Only if they're perfect. I've never met anyone like you. Wise, intriguing, cute as hell, full of life. I just think we get on amazingly. Don't hate me for liking you.'

'I don't, I –'

She paused and looked at me. I read her eyes.

My heart shifted inside my chest.

I put my left hand under her soft chiselled chin and tilted her head upwards and I leaned in and kissed her full and tender on the lips and the taste of her lips got me a little drunk. It was gin and whisky and salt-air and cherry lipstick, it was her own delicious flavour pressing itself into my memory.

Our little physical togetherness gave me immediate insight into her sensual side, another personality. She kissed me with a slow hotness and then as she pulled away bit at my lip as if in anger. My skin tingled with unexpected joy. It was almost as if someone had spiked her drink. For whatever reason, a new, more instinctive Juliette was emerging.

I gave a happy sigh. I felt tearful, like I got a year's worth of bliss all at once. I was brimming over. I held her in a warm hug so she wouldn't see my tears.

Forget peoplewatching. *We* were people.

I wanted to say 'I'm yours' but I knew this would scare her off, so I just thought it loudly again and again and again as I held her against me, our hearts quckening and synchronising.

Heartbeats. Italy. Italy. *Italy*.

My God. At some point you have to face up to it, what it means. Be fair, show that side of things.

I was staying in the Hotel Mharsaili in Rome, near the Termini. This part of Rome was neither cheap nor decent, especially at night, and I had a discomforting feeling that the lack of home comforts made me feel somehow . . . comfortable. I was at peace in among that edginess, that sleaze.

A woman hit on me near the railway station. I'd been stepping into a café and I held the door open for an attractive woman on her way out. She beamed at me, her cheekbones round and shining and she said 'Grazie' in an un-Italian accent. Christ, she looked like one of the happiest people I'd seen in my life. A Bodhisattva of a woman.

Inside, I ordered an espresso and drank it standing at the bar, feeling like a local despite my peelywally skin. I looked about, memorising distinctive Roman body languages for future characters and I happened to turn and look at the door – no, it wasn't a chance happening, I glanced across because I was still impressed that such a cheerful beauty had incorporated my presence in her own, superior life.

There she was. She was smiling and waving at me through a porthole-like window in the café door. I looked around. Everyone else was oblivious to her. I looked at the porthole again. She grinned and gestured.

I pointed at my chest and mouthed, 'Me?'

She nodded, broadened her smile and beckoned me to come outside.

I looked about – I may even have checked for some hidden prankster cameras – and left some money on the bar and strolled as casually as I could towards that portal which, it seemed to me, was opening up to an actual proper holiday adventure.

Outside she spoke to me in accented Italian and I guessed she was from somewhere in the Middle East. Maybe. I couldn't tell. Nor understand her. She spoke in broken Italian and I managed a few stuttered words of English. As she addressed me in a seductive, almost impassioned way, I couldn't help noticing the greasy wrapper of dripping fast food she had in her left hand. I couldn't even tell what sort of food it was. As her brief monologue came to an end, I gave the international sorry-I-don't-understand-you shrug, emphasising the sorry part of it with a zigzag smile.

She said something else and started moving away so I followed her. She stopped and – I flinched – she put the wrapper of food down on top of a bin. We were standing at a street corner in the warmish evening and she was using a bin as a table. This beautiful woman whose curly black hair shone under the streetlight with cinematic grace. We spoke at each other for a while, I can't remember what I said, mostly I think I just asked her inane questions. I have no idea what she said to me.

31

As we 'conversed', from time to time she raised the bag of food and bit into – ah, it was a kebab, positively Scottish with grease. At length – and I'm embarrassed at how long it took me to pick up on this – I realised she was a prostitute. Who was interested in procuring my business. I ran a hand through my hair. I was upset that I'd let myself believe this sublime-looking woman had any genuine interest in me. I was lonely, holidaying on my own.

I was dismayed that a woman had to sell herself on the street to make money for . . .

I scanned the street. Right enough, there were plenty rough, drug-dealer types hanging outside the Termini station across the road. Pimps.

Was I tempted?

I'm always tempted.

I gave her some money, not much, and walked away.

She called something out to me through a mouthful of food, but I didn't give her so much as a backwards glance.

.

Later that night, as I lay on 'my' bed in the Hotel Mharsaili trying not to think of all the thousands (I guessed) of people who had slept in it, I kept shifting around, convinced the bed was writhing with tiny insects. Grubs. The room had a thick dusty odour as though it had never been aired. Tired and half-alert, I kept a foggy, sepia-tinged night-light on. Something had swooped with a rushing of wings outside the window earlier. A bat, I think. It gave my heart a judder that wouldn't subside.

I thought now about the prostitute and now about Juliette. I told myself it was consideration of Juliette that had prevented me from being physical and/or intimate with that beautiful woman. I told myself twice.

The door burst open. Ugly fluorescent white light flooded the room. A silhouette appeared, splitting the light into substance.

?

A curly-haired woman swayed into the bedroom. Everything dark. She walked slow and confident, side to side, made you think her hips were smiling, made you think she knew you or wanted to. Short denim jacket and a tiny, skintight skirt. Those thighs were shaped by a lustful God's hand. As she strolled into the room she kicked the door shut behind her.

Now I could see her better. It was the prostitute.

I quivered with what I hoped and feared was anticipation. Which is, I guess, what anticipation is anyway. I gulped a dry swallow of insecurity.

She was a woman whose beauty moved and terrified me. I was a man who felt wrong and odd and undeserving and overdeserving and woebegone and free.

I trembled and watched as she walked towards me, her hips swaying from there all the way to over here, her skirt and jacket clinging like my tactile intense thoughts.

She moved towards my bed. I lay there, mouth too dry to speak, eyes unable to blink. She almost hypnotised me.

She stopped right there in her high heels. Looked at me. Her expression was almost neutral, but her dark hair and incomplete smile shared a dusky quality, something that was sultry and possessive.

She held my gaze.

I tried to speak.

She swivelled her hips, slapped her left, no left to me, her right hand on her right buttock. My mind sizzled. She whipped her hand back out from there and held a strip of silver shimmering in the half-light.

She gazed at me.

I croaked a 'What?' and a 'No.'

She was going to fucking stab me.

She stepped towards the bed. She twirled the blade – it was a short knife, like a fish-knife, slim and sharp – in her hand. My heart thrummed. How would I defend myself? What Carabinieri or whatever they're called in this place would believe me?

I thought, I always thought, I would get through this life without killing someone. (I also believed that I would marry a beautiful woman whom I met in a heroic situation; the girl wouldn't marry me simply because I saved her life, but because divine fate brought us, the right couple, together, preordained and deserving of one ajoyousnother.

Yes. Well.

In reality this is a world of mental and physical sickness and it is an ingenious symptom of that sickness to believe otherwise.)

My face collapsed. It fawned. Guess I looked like a coward. I stared at her and she gave the tiniest of smirks. She knew what I didn't. If my life depended on it, I would have fallen out of bed and cowered down at her knees, her ankles, and kissed her feet and promised her I love you, I love you, kissed her feet, kissed her toes, kissed her smooth shins, kissed her feet again, kissed her with thirsty lips pressing soft into the guessed-at familiarity of her warm skin.

She gave me a look.

And she raised the little knife like a point worth quietly making and she looked at me and she smiled at my chest and she smirked at my pulling my knees towards my chest and she plunged

in an amber flash

that knife towards her heart.

It was too slow and it was too fast. It was painful to watch, it was horrendous to endure and impossible not to. I flailed on the bed. Incapable. She stuck that fucking tearful knife into herself.

I mean – what? I cried. I cried out. She had plunged it towards her heart, that sharp blade, and it almost stuck, it bounced against her ribcage, her beautiful how many men ugly men ugly-minded and ugly-bodied saw that lovely chest, and it failed right there, that knife skidded across her breastbone, and she flinched, she aimed, hard, she felt it like a mistake, almost embarrassed, she grabbed that knife again, held it out in front of her, further, she held it out in front like it was a sword and I pleaded in my eyes at least I mean in my heart and everywhere and in my eyes I swear it was very visible, my voice wouldn't work right, I tried to cry out 'No' and she stabbed I mean first she pushed the knife far away from her, way far, so you thought nothing would happen, what did it mean, then she pushed it from her point of view and hers is the only one, yanked it hard towards her and how how can I mean that fast how can anyone, you try it, pull a knife that will kill you, any knife, blade, pull it towards you fast and hard you can't you can't you can't.

She did.

The knife spliced her skin, it bit into her heart – she cried, her cry was blood, she gurgled, she cry-gurgled blood, I wanted to save her, I thought I felt her pain, she started to die, she knew it, I knew it.

She stabbed herself in the heart.

People do this all the time, but not literally.

I felt it, too. I fainted.

•

A bland white ceiling. They could at least have painted a 'Welcome Back' sign on it, or the face of God or some such. Or a telly, they should show films up there, but only nice ones. Laughter. Best medicine.

A woman was stroking my left hand. Itchy. I withdrew my hand. A man with a sledgehammer was rearranging my skull from the inside. Ouch ouch ouch ouch.

A soft, darklytwinkling voice. 'Can you hear me? Keep those lovely green eyes open – don't you go back to sleep now. Look at me.'

The nurse was in her mid-thirties, and she had the kind of purity in her face that advertises make-up. Something in her honesty and in her deep blue eyes lowered my defences. Her soft red lips wreathed themselves into a wry smile. She seemed quite at ease with herself. Her presence – she was calm in her movements – gave me permission to think things would be all right. I stared at her until my eyes blurred over.

I realised she'd been asking me something. The pounding in my head was loud and distracting. The sharp beeping coming from somewhere close by didn't help. I sighed and it came out like a groan.

'Can you tell me your first name?'

I paused. My lips and tongue were cracked and dry, like I'd spent all night eating salt. Night? Or day?

'W-water.'

She poured a glass of water from the bedside pitcher and held the plastic glass to my mouth. I could literally feel the cold water coursing its way through my body. Giving me strength.

She wiped dribble from the corners of my mouth with a practised tissue.

'Th-thanks.'

'Do you know what day it is? No? D'you remember what happened, pal?'

I frowned. 'Pain. My head.'

'The doctor'll be along shortly, when he's finished with his last patient. Or cured him, whichever's easier. So, can you think for me – what happened?'

I concentrated. 'Axe. Axe. Accident.'

'Axe axe accident,' she echoed, in a friendly familiar way. 'More of a car–bike accident.'

'H-how's my bike?'

She gave a little spray of tinkly laughter. A droplet of her saliva landed on my lips, giving me a tiny dirty *frisson* of bliss. My lips tingalingled. I licked my lips and my heart tingalinged. 'I'm sure your bike's going to be fine. It's down in X-ray as we speak. Seriously, I'm sure that you're going to be fine too.'

She leaned in closer. 'You're very lucky, you know. You'll need to look after yourself more carefully.' Her blue eyes looked so far into mine I wondered if she could picture the sledgehammer guy. Her face was solemn. 'Most people only get one chance at life.'

The seriousness left her face and curiosity took its place. 'Hey, what are you laughing at?'

True enough, a low gurgling was slowly machinegunning through my vocal chords.

'I can't remember my own name.'

She smiled. 'You can't? Says on your chart your name's Egbert.'

I gurgled louder.

'Right, mister – I'll go and see where the doctor is hiding.' She got up and gave my hand a warm and gentle squeeze.

◆

I paid the sullen taxi driver and limped through a mild fog towards the theatre entrance. My feet were sore, a little twisted because of being forcibly unclipped from the pedals as I did my unwitting Superman halfway across London Road. My head felt like the early days of a civil war.

Paul 'the Jewel' Blinkbonny, the director, stood there sucking on a cigarette. A few feet from him, scowling at the smoke, was Mac, whom he must have buttonholed on the way in. As a little wisp of blueish grey smoke drifted through the fog, the top half of Mac, who's asthmatic, did a slight twisty, hula-hoop movement to dodge it. Writers are crazy.

He was first to recognise me. I was avoiding mirrors, but Nurse Stevenson had told me exactly what sort of sight I was. My feet were at an odd angle, my body movements jerky and puppet-like and I had a thick white bandage wrapped round my pulsing head. I'd had a go at itching the epicentre of the pain and the bandage had retreated a little and exposed a few millimetres of the wound. Nurse Stevenson had refused to sort it. I still didn't know her first name, but I had to go back in a couple of weeks to get the stitches removed. Nine of them.

'It's Jekyll and Hyde, Robert,' said Mac, 'not Frankenstein.' Ever the smartass.

Paul blanched. 'Is this a joke?' he asked with an icy stare.

I grimaced. 'Hardly.'

Mac gave a whistle and shook his head. '*Italy* did this to you? You need to take fewer holidays.'

'Edinburgh. Yesterday – no, day before. Been in hospital. Car sideswiped me.' I sniffed. 'My bike's ruined.'

Mac, who also rides bikes, winced. He looked me up and down. 'Damn. Well, hey, you're not in any condition for riding just now anyway.'

Paul had recovered his composure. He stroked his chin. 'The question is: are you in any condition for acting?'

'Course I am,' I snapped. 'I checked myself out of hospital early for this.'

Paul and Mac exchanged a look.

'Maybe we should get back in,' said Mac.

'Yeah,' said Paul with a slow nod. He smeared his cigarette butt into the dead-cancerstick grill.

'D'you want us to carry you in?' Mac asked, with a straight face. Paul the Jewel is that small and skinny and precious you can't imagine him carrying so much as a heavy thought. Mac raised an inquisitive eyebrow at me. You can never tell with that smartass.

'We'll introduce you to Woolfe,' said Paul, leaning his negligible weight against the door.

Mac pushed it hard, held it open.

'Oh,' I said, 'and I'm fine, by the way, thanks for asking.'

＊

As I shuffled my way into the rehearsal room behind Paul and Mac, the heavy, soundproof door swung back and hit me. I turned splitsecondswift and raised two hands in alarm, but I was more shocked by the fear-flashback this mundane collision triggered than the actual door-in-faceness of it all. For an eyeblink instant, the door was a grey concrete road and I was flying towards it.

The door was a door and my hands took the feeble-after-all brunt of its momentum. *I'm getting scared of doors*, I thought to myself, both disturbed by and marvelling at this absurdity.

The next shock was the change in atmosphere a little respite had brought to rehearsals. Wow. If anything, the simmering tensions in the cosy little auditorium had worsened. My fellow actors – Juliette, Drew and Harris – were strafed with practised casualness over the comfy red chairs of the front row, as if both nonchalant and chalant. I'll deign to get on the stage, they seemed to say, if someone *begs* me . . . and when I do, I'll be dynamite.

Their un-idle-seeming chatter carried through the muffly bandaging that tickled at my ears and I heard the following as I hirpled in:

'. . . done a runner, I reckon.' This was in the cocky Glaswegian voice Harris Gorebridge reverts to when he isn't speaking to someone who can give him a job. Stupid, handsome Harris who will one day be stupid, formerly handsome Harris. You never feel comfortable with Harris. One of his eyes always looks out of focus.

'. . . riddance, 'cause the Wolfman's got it all s–' Drew MacMerry's hissy Corstorphine preciousness cut off the moment his boyish doe-eyes clocked me.

Juliette, I noticed, said nothing. She looked at me for a moment and a mixture of concern and revulsion confused her face. Confused mine, too. She looked glossy and immaculate as ever, but something about her was different.

And something else was wrong. Something was missing. Someone? Yes? No?

✦

'All right, darlings,' Paul's high wheedling RP started up. He clapped two soft sharp hands together in his best Noël Coward. 'Let's take a moment. Undivided attention, thank you.' He stepped up on to the low stage, his hands flapping like manacled doves. Once he reached centre-stage, his well-groomed waif-like body struck a pose. His eyes took on a forced look of wistfulness and peered into a non-existent distance for a moment. His nostrils flared. When Paul says he got into all this because he loves drama, he isn't kidding.

I eased myself – nothing easy about it – into the seat beside Juliette. Might have been my imagination, but she seemed to stiffen as I sat down. She looked me over, flashed a quick actorial smile and directed her gaze back towards Paul.

Drew leaned towards me and sucked air in through his teeth the way a tradesman does when you ask for an estimate. He said, quoting the play in a deliberate stage whisper that reeked of cheese-and-onion crisps, 'You have a strong feeling of deformity, though I couldn't specify the point.' He paused a beat. 'Oh wait, yes I can. It's your bashed-up head, your screwy legs and the fact your nose has grown a nose.'

Everyone laughed. Even Juliette couldn't stifle a snort of cruel laughter. My face burned red. 'Fuck you,' I said before I could stop myself. I mentally kicked myself, the mere thought of which set my feet throbbing with renewed pain.

'The hell happened to you anyway?' said Harris.

Paul gave me a condescending nod. How gracious of you to allow me to speak, I thought, you passive-aggressive motherjumper. One of these days I'll tear you into pieces and feed you to your own ego.

Paul 'the Jewel' Blinkbonny: a magazine-addict, always dressed younger than he could ever get away with. One fine day a slew of glossy sleb-scandal magazines came spilling out of his shoulder bag, impossiblebreasted airheads flouncing among dark stiffbacked Shakespeares and Chekhovs and Ibsens. That's when I began in my mind calling him Paul the Dual. Putting the dual in individual since nineteen-canteen. Still, at least he wasn't as precious as Luffness, a lecturer/director we had at drama school, a man so sensitive he once brushed his teeth to meet a puppy.

I noticed Mac was sitting off to the side on his own with a notebook open, observing, scratching with his pen, that remote fire as usual burning behind silent eyes. Yes, Mac. If you want people to think you're deep, just sit there saying nothing, occasionally smirking, you *fake*. I read eyes like you read plays.

I cleared my throat. Everyone's attention focused on me like a dress rehearsal. I shook my head, which sent the room spinning a little. Maybe it was the disrespect they were giving me, maybe it was the lack of attention from Juliette, maybe it was just the actor in me, well, *acting* up, but anyway I decided that to maximise the effect I should shrug the whole thing off. That way I could win some kudos here, reverse the situation.

'Almost got killed,' I said in a matter-of-fact tone. Deliver a dramatically loaded line with well-pitched everyday carelessness and you will exude coolness. 'My cardiac very nearly arrested. Pissed bus driver thought red was green. No biggie.'

I am the new Brando. Without the belly. And alive.

'I thought you said a car sideswiped you,' said Mac.

'No, a bus, I said.' I coughed. 'There was a car there, too. Cars. Lots of them.'

'You poor thing,' said Juliette (or was it the actor in her?) She patted my arm. Once. Then looked back towards Paul, though I could tell she was thinking about me. Surely.

'Is your bike okay?' said Drew, either seriously or not.

Drew MacMerry does part-time modelling, including some for gay magazines we're not supposed to know about because he's straight. One of them dropped out of Paul's ridiculous shoulder bag in the early days of rehearsals. Only Juliette and I saw it; it amused us no end. I was all for posting the naked pictures of Drew's skinny staple-punctured butt all around the rehearsal room, but Juliette confiscated the magazine and banned me from even mentioning it again, damn it. Morals kill fun.

Drew is irritating; he's always eating crisps, talking with his mouth full, crunching synthetic smells into your ear. Behind his back we call him Eat, Drink and MacMerry. He's a liar, too. A hypocrite. Maybe every actor is. Maybe I am. Maybe everyone is.

It's his manner of hypocrisy that sets your teeth and mind and patience on edge. His is a slimy hypocrisy. You can see the slime oozing behind those big shiny brown eyes.

'Okay, undivided attention,' said Paul. 'I'm sure Robert will regale you with the full story later. Now. There's repercussions, there's announcements. We need to –' He paused; even the hand-birds froze. 'Where's the Wolfster – uh, where's Woolfe?'

'This was the day,' Juliette spoke up, 'he was doing that film thing. He said he'd cleared it with you at the interview.' She hesitated. 'The Sean Connery movie, he's young Sean in the flashback?'

'Oh,' said Paul. 'Yes. Yes. I'd forgotten about that. Damn. Yeah.'

'We got Roberto here back. How does this all figure?' said Drew.

'Who's afraid of the wolf?' I said and the words spat themselves out with a bitter edge I hadn't intended.

'Right. As I say . . .' Paul and the birds resumed. 'Now, Robert hasn't been aware that during his holidays and his – uh, his escapades, his unfortunate escapades – we've had further production issues.'

'What's new?' I said, *sotto voce*, but I knew *something* was up. I shifted in my seat. A cold searing pain knifed at my chest.

'We had *horrendous* funding and logistical issues. There were emergency meetings with all our funders – I mean, I wish *I* could have been burnishing my bronze in Italy, but there was a lot of stress and a lot of decision-making. I fought for each and every one of you. But we did have to make some compr – we sought difficult creative solutions to our obstacles.

43

'One, of course, was that we had a play here that has no prin-cipal female roles. Not Mac's fault, of course, he didn't write the original. Though he probably wishes he had –' Paul waved a bird at Mac.

Mac said, blithe and brisk, 'I dunno, with all the rewrites I'm thinking of giving it all up and becoming a lighthouse engineer.'

'Rewrites?' I sat up, alert. My spine screamed. 'Ow – um – I got – I've got new lines to learn?'

An awkwardness filled the room. My esteemed colleagues discovered a fascination with footwear.

'Well, yes,' said Paul. 'And no. As I was saying, we questioned if the play really spoke to the females who make up at least half our audience. We decided that no, it didn't. It was a natural progression from there to rewriting Lanyon as a female char-acter and to offer that role to Juliette. Playing merely a maids-ervant and a trampled girl was hardly appropriate to an actor of her standing.'

Juliette smiled at the floor.

A fearful happiness began to wash over me. But wait – 'Wait. Where's Phil, then?' I *liked* Phil.

'Well, very regretfully, among the changes, we had to release Philip to pursue other opportunities. I'm sure he'll be in touch with you, especially when he hears –' Paul stalled. 'Anyway, owing to the pressures I mentioned, we had to bring rehearsals forward.'

Everything grew very still.

'Robert, we tried *everything*. We *phoned* you. We *emailed* you. We went *round to your flat* to see if you were back. Not once, *many* times. We needed you here. To resume rehearsals. Where was your mobile?'

'I lost it,' I lied. Actually, I'd hurled it into the Tiber. It was sleeping with the Italian fishes.

'No one knew where you were.'

'But I told Juliette –' I looked at her; she almost imperceptibly turned away.

'We knew you were in Italy. Italy's a big place. Don't you check your emails?'

'Not when I'm on *holiday*. Plus, you know I'm not online at home.' Well, Juliette, at least, knew this. 'So.' I tried to clear my head, which was thumping with pain. 'What's going on?'

\

'We tried everything.' A note of false regret and affected pain crept into Paul's voice. More than ever, I reflected on how disingenuous Paul was. I wanted to tear his passive side from his aggressive side and knock them together until they were mush.

Jeez, I've got to calm – wait, he was talking in a Very Serious Voice and I'd tuned out.

'. . . need to remind you that you were not *on holiday*, you were on paid release, a contractual element that comes with certain conditions – conditions you breached, incidentally. You knew you only had time off unless or until we called you back in. That is in the contract you signed on day one. You're meant to be available at a day's notice, a single day. None of the others went to Italy.'

I tried breathing slowly through my nose. Didn't work, made me dizzy. My blood pressure was building, deepening the pain in my head. I said, louder than I intended, 'Am I *fired*? I'm meant to be the fucking lead roles. Am I, are we, no longer part of this production?'

'No, but you have missed some important rehearsals and so we talked yesterd–'

'Yesterday I was in a bloody coma. The only person speaking to me was Saint Peter. He was wearing a goddamn bandana, singing "Welcome to Paradise". "No," I said, "Paradise is on hold, I got a major production to do, I'm a fucking human abacus, there's so many people counting on me."'

'Yes,' the Jewel said with a patronising smile. 'Slight touch of hyperbole there.' Like he was one to talk, the spotlight-hogging bird-manacling hypocrite. 'You're still part of this production. But we have a new dynamic here and indeed a new, still evolving script. We've got a couple of weeks' rehearsal which you've *missed* and we've got a new artiste on board, whose name I'm sure you've heard –'

'Heard nothing but,' I muttered. I was beginning to hate this guy I'd never met. So what, I never met Hitler either.

Oh. I'd missed more bullshit.

'. . . in the industry. Where he's gathering a *very* enviable reputation and truth be told he's just signed up with the Gods & Monsters Agency of London and LA, and I don't need to tell you what that means. This might even be his last stage work in Scotland. You'll meet Woolfe tomorrow and I'm sure you'll get on . . . *famously*.' He looked around as a smirk spread over his fizzog. 'Maybe he'll bring Sean along for coffee.'

The others gave a desultory spatter of obsequious laughter.

But I was struggling to contain my fury. 'You're giving a wolf my part and I'm, what . . . do I heat up his dog food? Comb the fur on his hands? I mean, what . . . do you shave him for the Jekyll scenes?' I was now standing on my unsteady feet, shaking with anger at Paul – and at myself for being so immature. I knew I'd taken things too far. Maybe that bang on the head had affected me more than I knew.

A silence held court for a moment or two . . . and passed its judgement.

'He was going to be more like an understudy,' said Paul.

Jeez. I slithered down into my seat. Even my internal organs cringed in humiliation.

'But, as I said, just as the script is ever evolving, so is the production as a whole. I'm going to keep you both on the payroll at the moment as part of the acting talent. We're borrowing some scenery from a recent production of *Dracula's Caledonian Massacre*, which is, thank God, saving us an absolute fortune. I don't think anyone can say fairer than that. We don't even know yet if you're up to doing the part . . .'

'I'm fine,' I said, but in my eagerness to respond I swallowed my breath the wrong way and brought on a mild splutterfit.

'. . . plus we only have Woolfe here if a certain film role he auditioned for doesn't come through.'

The others looked at each other. This was clearly news to them.

'I've got an idea,' Harris piped up. 'Why not get Woolfe to play Jekyll and Rob to do Hyde? Perfect.'

'Hmm,' said Paul. 'I don't think that would work. Let's just see how things unfold. We're holding them both for the time being – can't afford *not* to, since their futures are so . . . unde-cided. But, no. We can't have them both. Jekyll must be Hyde. That's the whole point.'

＼

Paul remembered how much passion he had invested in the sound of his own voice, so his speech resumed and it was some time before it drew to a fluttering close. 'Well, that's enough for one day, especially since Woolfe isn't here,' he announced. 'Mac, you do some work on that second act, and you lot go over your lines and get some rest. No trips to Italy, mind.'

I bared my teeth in a sarcastic smile. He continued, unfazed. 'Me, I'll chase up wardrobe for Juliette's dresses and think about blocking the climax. We'll meet up here bright-tailed and bushy-eyed tomorrow morning nine-thirty sharp. We're behind schedule so I want everyone on their best form. Right – vamoose. Or *arrivederci* in your case, Roberto.'

On the way out I hobbled fast enough to catch hold of Juliette's arm – just as someone grabbed my own elbow. I turned to see Mac's eyes boring into me. At the same time Juliette was saying, 'Don't *grasp me*.'

'Hang on – Juliette, can we talk?'

'Um . . . Sure.'

'At least *try* to restrain your enthusiasm.'

'I said yes. Just remember, I have this whole new role I'm learning, so we'll need to keep an eye on the time.'

I looked back to Mac, who asked, 'How's your improv?' As I made to fill him in on my considerable talents in that field he held up a sheaf of paper. 'Cause otherwise, just thought you might like a *script*, is all, what with it being entirely rewritten.'

'Oh.' I blushed. 'Yeah.' I caught Paul out of the corner of my eye shoot a disapproving look this way. 'The ole bang on the noggin. I'm not quite right.'

'There's a hundred answers to that,' said Mac, 'all of them too easy.'

As I took the script, he placed a warm hand on my shoulder. 'Robbie,' he said, in a softer tone which seemed to suit his weird accent. 'Look after yourself.'

'Yeah, yeah. I will. You too, man. Take it easy. But do take it.'

'Take what?'

'. . .'

'Anyway, Rob. I mean it. You gotta take better care of yourself. There's a lot at stake here. You can't lose this. Most people only get one chance at this.'

\

Juliette and I went to the Festival Theatre on Nicolson Street for lunch and for, we both knew it, a big chat. We sat by the huge windows, where so much life and light poured through. Here we could feel like the observing and the observed, both sides of the cinema screen at once. Juliette had had a haircut since I last saw her; the long Bohemian straggles were styled into a glossy bob that struck me as inappropriate for the Jekyll and Hyde era. She did look beautiful, though – more so than ever. Her blue eyes had a drowsy shimmer that made me want to hug her tight, warm, long. Right now, a heart-synchronising hug would cure all my troubles.

She gave her cough and slight twitch of the head that meant *Stop staring*. I turned and looked out the window. There was a gentle fog, so mild you had to strain to see it. The Southside day was alive with movement, unspoken inner dramas, sheer mental essences simmering beneath routine mundanities.

Peoplewatching. An artist's prerogative. Every actor's a voyeur. Elderly pastel women with little tartan shopping trolleys and charity shop carrier bags shuffled past. In pairs and larger gaggles tall white-smiling students in stripey scarves strode through life as though it were an easy privilege. Tense young mums sucked hard on cigarettes and shoved shoogly prams, the excitement of a trip uptown fading as it happened. Crowded with loneliness, a bus wheezed past in a fug of exhaust fumes, its driver an emblem of misery: overweight, dead-eyed, grouchy. Following the same script and the same route in the same circumstances every day. Who could live like that? Thank God there are people who do. They make society flow. I was just about to say, 'I hope that driver's got an absolute pleasure-drenched pair of acrobatic twin wives back home,' when Juliette asked, 'Was there a doctor on the bus?'

I tried to think of the punchline. 'Eh?'

'The bus.' She pointed a listless cherry red fingernail at a number 33. It was urging everyone who looked at it to go and see a musical that was on at the Playhouse. I wondered how many people would come to see our show. 'One of those things. Your nemesis.'

I deflated a little inside. Lying was something I reserved for other people, not Juliette. 'Uh, no. "Doctor on the bus" – sounds like a 1970s sitcom. Nah, I had to hitch a ride in a meatwagon. I'm lucky to be alive.'

She gave a half-smile. 'Drama queen.'

'No, really. Listen –'

Juliette shifted and brightened. I turned, vexed; the waitress had arrived as suddenly as if she'd popped up out of the floor using stage trickery. I absently looked for a trapdoor while Juliette asked for scrambled egg on a toasted bagel and a decaf cinnamon latte. I ordered the same, to emphasise how alike we were.

Silence.

Or did ordering the same make me look indecisive and weak? And decaf? That definitely made me look weak.

Silence.

Her reflective, me agitated.

'What's happening?' I said at last.

She shrugged. 'About what?'

'You act like you don't really want to be here.'

'I act like an actor with lines to learn so I can act my part well and so gain more acting work. That's how I act.'

'Did everyone get brainwashed while I was away? Does no one give a damn I was wiping my half-broken feet on the welcome mat at death's door?'

She sighed. 'You know, you don't half overdramatise things. Save the histrionics for the stage. Look, don't take this the wrong way, but – you got knocked off your bike. Same thing happened to me when I was eleven.'

'I hardly think . . .'

'My daddy kissed it better and got me a new bike, one that was bigger, wasn't pink and didn't have pony stickers on it. You'll get over it, Rob. You're shaken up, you have a little pain . . .'

'You know nothing of the pain I'm in, lady.'

I regretted it the moment I said it. Must've picked it up from a film. Actor's curse – too much empathy, too little remembering who you're supposed to be.

'*Lady*?' She spat the word back at me.

'I didn't mean it like that. I just – a little sympathy wouldn't go amiss. I mean, here I am, back from holidays, a hug all unwrapped in my arms, ready to wrap around you . . .'

'Pair of scrambled egg bagels, here we go.' The waitress beamed at Juliette, even as she plonked a plate down in front of me. 'Would you like your lattes now or after the meal?'

'We'll just have the coffee now, thanks. Thank you.' Juliette mirrored the waitress's smile.

We ate in silence. I couldn't taste the food – through angry frustration or as a result of my injuries, I didn't even care.

Laying my knife and fork on the plate together in the official finished position, I tried again. 'How have rehearsals been going?'

Juliette waited till she'd chewed her mouthful thirteen times then swallowed. She always did this, so she could get more nutrients from her food, and therefore eat less and therefore stay slim and therefore get more acting work. She dabbed a napkin at the corner of her mouth. 'Mmm. It was a bit intense for a while. When we first got called back, there was a chance the whole production was going to be shelved. I thought Paul would have a coronary.'

'I can imagine.' Truth is, I *could* imagine it and I confess the image pleased me. Just for a moment, then guilt pangs started like a headache. No, it was a headache.

'And no one could get a hold of you, and there were all these rewrites. I really did try everything to get in touch with you, by the way. While you were lying on some Italian beach –'

I half-stood up, sending the chair scraping away behind me. '*What* did you say?'

'While you were sunning – sit down, you're embarrassing yourself – sunning yourself on some Italian beach, we were working our asses –'

'Oh God. I'm sorry.' I retrieved my chair, plomped into it.

'Everything okay with your food and with – everything else?' The waitress had reappeared.

'Great, thanks,' said Juliette. She nodded her head in my direction. 'He's had an accident, gets a little . . . worked up.'

The waitress gave me an uncertain look, took Juliette's plate away and left mine where it was.

'I'm really sorry. It must be these bloody bandages. I thought you said, "While you were lying on some Italian bitch . . ." '

The word hung in the air like a vision of something broken.

Juliette sighed, shook her head a couple of times.

The thought struck me that she wouldn't feel the slightest bit jealous if she believed I *had* slept with an Italian girl. A heaviness came over me; I slumped forwards on the table.

'Maybe you should get a bus – well, a taxi – home. Best stay away from buses, eh. Get some rest. Go to bed with a good play.'

'Yeah. Wanna come read it with me?'

Her look gave me all the answer I needed.

'How is the play now? And what about this Woolfe character?'

Juliette bristled. 'What about him? He's a bloody good actor. They're saying he's the new James McAvoy. And the thing is, it's plausible.'

'I feel like I've been cast away. I'm a castaway from the cast. Usurped. The good daughter from *King Lear*.' I gathered a little mental strength. 'Is he good-looking?'

'What?' Juliette made a laughsplutter sound.

'Is he better-looking than me?'

She laughed. 'You, uh – you're not exactly looking at your best right now.'

My head was spinning and throbbing at the same time. The dizzying revolutions were getting worse. I patted the bandage.

'You just put some scrambled egg on your bandage.'

I wiped it away. 'Symbolises my scrambled head.'

'Seriously,' she said, relaxing a little, 'I think we're all, like, if it was that bad you'd be kept in hospital. *Are* you exaggerating? I mean, we never know with you. What's the pain like, on a scale of one to ten?'

'The feet usually four, rising to six when I sit down, strangely enough. The head eight, rising to nine when I think of how the play has disintegrated or evolved without me and hitting ten whenever I think of you.'

I held my breath.

She sighed.

Put her jacket on.

Stood up.

'Then don't think of me.' She started to walk away.

I got up too, followed her, puppy-eyed, desperate. '*Wait.*
Juliette!'

The waitress appeared, genie-like, as was her habit, mildly
alarmed this time. 'Um, traditional to *pay* for food round these
parts, *sir.*'

'Your name isn't Jeannie, by any chance?' I gave her more
than enough, more than more than enough. 'Keep the change.'

'Thanks. And no. Bye.'

I hobbled out into the noisy grey world of grannies with
soup tins and students with egos. Like breaching the fourth
wall.

'Juliette.'

She turned.

'I heard someone's throwing movies. Let's go catch one.' I'd
practised this line, but it didn't work in real life the way it did in
fantasy. 'C'mon. We'll study acting. Contemplate character arcs.
Play the mouth-popcorn version of basketball.'

'Rob. You have a script to read.'

'Yeah, but –'

'And which you've left in there.' She indicated the glass
facade; inside, the waitress was holding up some papers. 'Go get
it. Read it. And just – take it easy. But do take it.'

'Take what?'

She leaned in to hug me goodbye, skilfully deflecting my kiss.

＼

The waitress looked at me as she held out the script. 'Don't you
break that girl's heart.'

'*Pardon?*' I snapped, incredulous.

'Interesting play, I said. Do you have a part?'

'Uh –'

'Sorry, kind of a daft question,' she said evenly, looking me up and down, 'when you're obviously playing Hyde.'

❜

Black cab after black cab swiped past as though I were invisible, and after about an hour I gave up and clambered onto a crammed, suffocating bus. By the time I got home I was weak with exhaustion. The pain in my head felt as though it were trying to beat itself unconscious. Yeah, no, my mind didn't seem right. I drank a glass of cold water and gulped down twice as many painkillers as I should have. For good measure, I did that twice. The pain eased not one bit.

I took a lukewarm shower in the hope that it would revive me long enough to read the new script. I made a mess of putting a new bandage round my head, but it was as good as I could manage. Maybe from some angles it would look like one of those bandanas rappers and dealers wear. I should maybe just buy a bandana and try to keep it clean and shit. Have *some* cred.

I lay down on the couch with a couple of lazy peanut-butter sandwiches and a mug of cinnamon tea. It felt good to lie down. My body gave an involuntary sigh.

My flat was small, meticulous, spare. I kept it as minimalist and unfussy as though it were uninhabited, or inhabited by a spy who is, in any case, only passing through. Whatever I used – a dishcloth, a bike spanner, a toothbrush – I hid away the moment I finished with it. It suited me to keep things simple, restrained.

True, some days it felt as though the flat were shrinking, especially the sink in the kitchen, and the bed linen seethed at nights with invisible insects, but I had neither time nor inclination to find a new place until the play had toured.

If it ever does.

I picked up the script. The first page read:

Jekyll & Hyde
by [peanut-butter smear]
Adapted from
Robert Louis Stevenson's
'The Strange Case of Dr Jekyll and Mr Hyde'

When I leafed over to the next page the typing no longer made sense. The black ink marks swarmed on the page like silent flies. Every letter was fidgeting around. I tried holding the restless text at arm's length. No good. Then at nose length (inadvertently banging new throbbing pain into my enlarged neb). The squiggles threw themselves around more dizzyingly than before, like a mad cloud of distressed bats. The disorientation in my brain sent queasy messages to my stomach. I squeezed my eyes. I rubbed them. I screwed them tight then opened them. Closed them again for a moment.

I ran the too-short film of my night with Juliette through my mind. I went through phases where this was a natural-as-breathing practice for me. Sometimes, I noticed with consternation, I put the wrong clothes on her, or I couldn't remember if she tucked a wisp of hair behind her ear at *this* point or *that*. Memory distorts, disconcerts. And when we die, odd little memes go on living, changing, lying.

Essences.

Parts.

We are merely players.

My mind flipped like a flying cyclist. Ha, I gurgled a laugh at that.

What about Juliette's possibly non-existent feelings for me? Did I hurt her that badly by not inviting her to Italy? How amazing were her natiform cheeks. Oh feck, and what about the script I needed to read. Take it easy.

I thought back to the first time I saw Juliette. Her eyes had rested on me for a moment when she appeared alongside Mac, that first day in the rehearsal room. She and Mac arrived as if they were . . . together. Impossible, any skilled observer of life such as I am could see that.

It was as if she had somehow recognised me and then her glance had moved to another part of the room. Had she taken an immediate interest in me? Or had she merely half-recognised my face from somewhere else in this tiny city? Had she turned away because she was flustered by the sudden strong feelings coming over her? Or had she just scanned a polite stranger-actor's face and then moved her attention to another polite stranger-actor's face?

Her slender body had a natural grace. Her hair was pure and black and glossy, like the pelt of a panther in moonlight.

I believed I'd sensed in her first look a wilfully subdued animation, a quickening borne out of sudden love. An almost imperceptible smile twitched once at her slim curvaceous lips, the kind of smile that is triggered by swift eyesacrosstheroom excitement.

Hmm. Yes . . . A not-quite-containable vitality had sent a quiver through her body, releasing itself in the shine of her eyes and her smile. She tried, near-consummate actor, to hold back her feelings, but her own body had betrayed her. Attractiveness will do this.

❧

Bzrp-bzrp. Bzrp-bzrp. I woke up to the sound of the alarm from the bedroom. At first I wondered, groggy-headed, why someone had tampered with my clock radio. Then I realised I was lying at a stiff unnatural angle on my living-room couch, fully clothed, dribbling, with a crumpled, peanut butter and saliva-stained script for a pillow.

It could *not* be morning.

I sat up, my head both woolly and sharply painful. Who knew you could have two headaches at the same time. I looked about; it was bright like daylight. My eyes were gritty, my neck cramped, my body weak. This, I thought with a sigh, must be what it's like to be old. You are not the same at twenty as you were at ten, not the same at forty as you were at twenty. Nothing's ever the same. Only get one chance at this.

It *was* light. I got to my aching feet and wobbled through to the bedroom. I slapped the nagging alarm clock quiet. I had slept for sixteen hours. Or forty?

I knew everything was wrong, as it always is when you sleep in, but I sat down there on the bed for a moment and begged for everything to be all right. Today was going to be crucial. A voice from within said, quoting a play we did at college in which I played a poet,

'Every morning we awaken
to some invisible clock in the sun
and the things we do not question
are manifold.'

Little sounds from antemeridian Edinburgh drifted up to my de-shrilled room, half-familiar in my ears. A car door slammed in the car park nearby: a not going to 'have a nice day' shop worker. *Screeeaoow*: a startled cat flipped out and scarpered over a wall. At another sound, I pictured a nearby grocer bowing to a shop, cranking an awning. A woman with a hacking cough cursed her life. An obnoxiously happy man pushing a rattly metal shopping trolley through the street yodelled a Scottish folk tune I couldn't recall.

All the people with their own little dramas.

I tried to smile and it hurt. I tried to frown and it didn't.

Oh well, I was alive, wasn't I? And all I had to do was impress Juliette and learn my new lines and pray the Woolfe guy was, as so many in his position are, overhyped and underwhelming.

᾿

'I only asked you to *read* the script, not beat it up,' said Mac, indicating my peanut butter-smeared script with his non-coffee-hand as we moved at my limping pace down the red hall towards the rehearsal room.

'My, uh, yeah, what happened was –'

'You fell asleep on your script?' He adopted a (pseudo?) solemn tone. 'Rob, did my script send you to sleep?'

'No, I uh – I was getting in character, y'know, getting physical with the lines and the movements.'

Mac took a measured sip of his cinnamon latte as if to draw my attention to how slowly we were moving. 'Uh huh.'

We walked along, him ambling *intensely*, the way writers will, me hirpling along, trying to act like someone who had digested a script, prepared for a role and slept well.

We stopped outside the door. 'Hey, Mac. Seriously. Tell me. How do I convince Paul the Jewel I'm the only one for this role?'

He shrugged, profoundly. That writerly air, again. 'You do what you do best.' His eyes locked on to mine. 'Did you read the script *at all*?'

'Read it? Man, I loved it! I've got so many questions about it.'

'Oh, questions. I like questions.' He looked bemused. 'What questions do you have regarding the script?'

I didn't have time to read much of the script in the taxi on my way here, but I did have some time to *prepare*. 'Well, for one thing, who *names* Edward Hyde? And for another – why does Hyde, who's evil and loving it, not to mention guilt-free, why does he decide to change back to Jekyll, when he's happy as he is being Hyde, no conscience?'

'Watch it or I'll invoke The Joke later.'

I serioused up. 'Don't even say that in jest. No, man, you took that too far.'

The Joke That Kills Careers was not, like calling Macbeth 'the Scottish play' (as if there's only one Scottish play) a questionable and ultimately lighthearted superstition. No, The Joke was guaranteed to kill any leading actor's performance of the play career-dead. Not a superstition but a powerful, hurtful reality.

'No smiles,' Mac said, 'no overacting, and I promise you success.'

I frowned, tried to read the situation. Again, I wasn't sure I quite got it. Was this a Jekyll and Hyde allusion or solid advice? Was Mac being a smartass or being himself? Or both?

Silence.

'Sometimes,' I said, 'I think you're the biggest fraud here. At least we *admit* we're actors.'

He grinned and reached over for the door handle. 'Maybe I speak enigmas, but I know you –' He narrowed his eyes, leered at me, ham-actor style. 'I know you to the soul.'

I snorted. 'Fucking writers.'

He pulled the door open. 'If you're serious about this part, quit lying to me and read the damned script.'

Giving a stagey little bow, he gestured for me to enter the rehearsal room. 'Focus. Be single-minded. No, wait. Be anything but single-minded. And watch your back with both your faces.'

❯

The rehearsal room that had, on the first day at least, felt so womb-like, where we would coax our creation into natural-seeming existence, like magic, now had a tired and uncomfortable atmosphere.

Paul had described the rehearsal area on the first day as 'the womb in which actors come into being, come fully into being'. It now had an atmosphere of potential and non-potential, of great hope quietly defeated, like a boxing ring in which two jaded boxers stumble about in a violent hug, tired and uncertain of who is stealing the bronze.

We all wanted the play to do well, I knew that. I was also aware that we all felt this: *I only want this play to do well if I am more crucial to its success than anyone else.*

My esteemed fellow thespians sat around chatting in the same studied poseurish manner they had yesterday. Paul was whispering with, I presumed, the great Woolfe.

Damn it, he *was* better-looking than me. But not by much. And on a good day, if I'd taken more time than usual to groom myself and dress well . . . it would be a close-run thing. And I have my killer charisma.

'Ah, Rob,' said Paul, turning to me all sweetly fragrant and false. 'Allow me to introduce Edward Woolfe. Woolfe, this is Robert Lewis. You both already know each other – by reputation at least.' An ambiguity hung in the air, triggered by that word *reputation*.

Don't be reconciled, I thought to myself. *You make your own life.*

61

I stumped a few inches closer and shook the Woolfe's paw. Hand, I mean. Let him speak first. Be the silent enigmatic stranger with the poker player's mystique. I appraised my adversary. About my height, and similar in build to me in that he had a well-toned body, his muscles efficient rather than bulky. I wondered what sport he did. Surely not cycling. Please, God. His hair was wavy and blond. His face was handsome, chiselled, the kind you see in . . . in the movies. The part of my stomach that harbours ill-will drowned some good-will.

Wait. Maybe he's too nice. Yes! *Maybe he'd be no good at Hyde.* A sheep in Woolfe's clothing.

If he were one of those rare actors who is handsome and talented, I'd kill him. If he were one of those actors who is handsome and talented and smart, I'd torture him first.

Bitterness set around me like a cast.

'Not like you to be overwhelmed,' said Paul, and at almost the same moment Woolfe said with a pleasant smirk, 'I heard you swapped one type of theatre for another?'

I didn't get it.

He spoke again. 'Operating theatre? Never mind. How are you, man?'

Was he being funny and reasonable and friendly? I doubted it. But maybe.

'No, *man*, I'm cool. I told them I had no time for operations. Show must go on.' Damn. A cliché. Fuckfuckfuck.

'Wai-wait,' said Paul. 'They wanted to operate?'

The room was hushed and staring at me.

'Noth-nothing serious,' I said, thinking fast. 'I have these genes, the ones like a starfish that make you self-heal quickly. This time next week, I'll be in peak condition, back on the bike and in full acting *flow.*'

'What kind of operation?' asked Juliette from behind, her voice spiced with a hint of disbelief, the cynical, not the wondrous, kind.

I turned to her. My neck flashed with pain. 'Ow.' I rubbed it, inwardly cursing myself. 'Good, the doctor said that's a sign it's healing. The, uh, neutrons in the nerves are responding.'

'Responding to what?' said Drew.

'The bullshit,' Harris muttered under his breath.

'Look, they wanted to operate on my feet,' I lied. 'Or they gave the option of letting the bones knit together by themselves, which is the natural way for it to correct itself, and also saves the NHS.'

'Well,' said Harris. 'Good for you and your magically healing heels.'

I turned my back on the three of them.

'R-ight,' said Paul. 'Let's get on with this. You've read the script?'

'Yeah yeah. *Love* it. Love all the changes.'

'We'll crack on with Act One Scene Four. Okay?' Paul minced up to the stage in that regimental way which means he's in No Messing mode.

A new strain of awkwardness entered the room. As though someone had mentioned The Joke That Kills Careers.

I swallowed, cleared my throat.

Rehearsals used to be *fun*. Well, more fun than this, anyway.

'What is it?' Paul halted; he looked like someone frozen in an amateur ballet stance.

'Um,' I said. 'Which one of us is going to play Jekyll and Hyde?'

Paul hesitated, looked us both over. 'We'll have Woolfe first because he's had longer to get acquainted with this draft of the script. You can pick up on what he does, then have a go at it in . . . in your own way, you know, with a feel for the rhythms and, and . . . Right, first positions everyone.'

)

Three *hours* later Paul granted me my turn. I'd sat in the front row all morning, interested at first to see how Woolfe handled the role. As I feared, he was good. *Very* good. But, I believed, not as good as I am. As I hunched there studying the rehearsals, I felt a wild malevolence build within me, like true freedom. If I could get back to good physical condition soon (*why* did I say that nonsense about miracle genes?), I could win this role – these roles – back. My improv skills had failed me earlier, and that stung, but I could cope with this challenge. Easy.

Woolfe's acting style was a little self-conscious for me. It was as though he already believed himself a huge star, which is commonplace among actors, but you should never let it negatively affect your performance. And he seemed to be relying on his perceived good looks and – the arrogance! – perceived *fame* to help win over the audience. Instead he should have focused on *being* the character. Characters, I mean.

Not acting, but being.

He was an actor *pretending* to be great and coming across as *vain*.

For the first time in too long I had a positive feeling about all this. Hell, maybe the guy and I could be friends, at least long enough for me to get to know his agent. His agent wasn't likely to be permanently over-the-hill and over-the-limit, a has-been who never *was*, potentially the agent of no more than my own misfortune. His agent probably had a contact book that wasn't full of defunct numbers and Resting-In-Peace names. His agent

64

probably had a phone that rang more than once a year. His agent probably had a bath more than once a year.

Yeah, the little Wolfboy could prove useful to me after all. Everything happens for some butterflying reason. I should just learn to relax about the direction my life and career (same thing) are taking. Career should be a verb rather than a noun. Or was it vice versa? Anyway, they were waiting for me. I'd had time enough to familiarise myself with the scene once I'd stopped worrying about Wolfboy.

I knew how to do this.

)

'All right, we'll imagine you've trampled Juliette to the ground. Rob, actually, I have to say, you look perfectly hideous – Hydeous, ha! – as you are. We might use some of these ideas in make-up. That's it, Juliette. You're a little girl, you've just been stomped and trampled by the disgusting monster, the likes of which you've never seen but in nightmares. Yes, you're young enough, you still believe in monsters and you truly believe he is one.

'Rob, give me more venom, give me simmering venom. You're in control, you emanate unearthly power and disgust and repugnance –'

'I almost think,' Harris chipped in, 'he should curb some of his natural repugnance.'

Juliette gave a splutter of outraged laughter which she converted to 'sobs' in character.

'Ha ha,' I muttered, 'not tedious at all.'

'Good, Juliette. Now focus, *focus*.' Paul clapped his fluttering hands, his voice scoldy and headmistressy. 'Okay, we'll take it from *Who the devil*.'

Harris-playing-Enfield took a tight grip of my collar. I tried to ignore the hurt. I couldn't allow my performance to be less than excellent. I couldn't give any of the others – but especially Woolfe – that satisfaction. Still, 'Enfield''s brute grip on my collar was noose-serious and I couldn't breathe right.

Harris adopted Voice Two. As an 'actor' he has his quiet voice which he uses for all emotions but anger and his loud voice which he reserves for rage. 'Who the devil do you think you are?' he bellowed, tightening the noose of his grip. 'You come charging through here like a Juggernaut, you trample this poor girl, this innocent girl, and you mean to take your leave without so –'

'And what concern,' I said, my voice foaming with derisive venom and a little serendipitous dribble, 'is it of yours?'

'Okay, Rob,' Paul interrupted, in his disheartening way. 'Just a tad bit more subtle there, please, don't you think? Most of your menace here is implicit, rather than explicit. Yes, you've trampled the girl, but to you that's a trifle. An *aura* of evil rather than – a chainsaw.'

My eyes bulged. Paul's ignorance and incompetence routinely infuriated me. I struggled to hold my anger in check. Don't get on Paul's bad side, not today.

'Sure thing. Subtle aura.' A thrill of anger simmered inside. It felt good to hold and tantalise that anger rather than release it straight out. Yes, the anger crescendoed nicely inside me. I kept it hidden; if anything, it seemed to get more powerful the more I held it in. I dizzied, like too much of a good thing. But my face was turning purple. The noose-grip.

Harris bellowed, 'I've got a good mind to trample *you* into the ground.'

'. . . kr . . . ktsh . . .' I managed but it was no use, I could no longer breathe, let alone speak. I raised a hand, flapped at Harris's insane grip, which was so tight I had literally stopped breathing.

'No, no, no. Drama, not melodrama, Rob, you know that.'

Harris let go. I fell to the floor, gasping for air.

)

After the overdramatic commotion of fussing over and picking up the 'clearly still affected' actor and talking about him as if he weren't in the room, came the even more dramatic kerfuffle of that actor persuading the Director and Talent that he was not only capable of continuing, he *insisted* upon it.

I hid my internal fuming like only the best actors can.

Not one of those idiots believed me that Harris's grip was so tight it would have choked a robot to death, oh no. When I mentioned the reason I'd collapsed, Harris shot me a contemptuous look that would have called me a bare-faced liar if looks could speak. I shot him one back that said: what kind of man are you, you traitorous moron?

When your friends are actors it's impossible to know where your relationships stand at any time, but that goes double when you know each other fairly well and it goes triple when you're fighting for limelight.

In this weird profession of manufacturing crises, the real drama is what goes on backstage. I can't watch a play without envisaging the real-life tensions going on among the cast when they're offstage.

We got back to rehearsing. As I stepped up on to the stage – yes, my feet, head and neck were pinching, throbbing and pulsating with nerve-tight pain, but I didn't let on – I caught sight of Woolfe out of the corner of my eye studying me in silence. I cleared my throat, a nervous gesture, which made me more nervous as I knew he'd seen it. Was he – was Woolfe making *notes*? The impertinence –

Harris made a show of 'grabbing' me about the collar as though I were made of God's own crystal. Still, I acted with restraint and dignity, thinking this was the style Paul's confused comments were aiming for.

We did the scene and I think I turned in a strong performance, regardless of the condescending looks the other actors gave me from time to time. I pretended I was being patronised by an ignorant, indifferent audience. Thus, the next time I took to the stage in front of such an audience I would be all the better prepared for it. What doesn't kill you . . .

At the end of the rehearsal, Mac surprised me by asking me round to his flat for a coffee that evening. I hesitated; I'd been planning to spend the evening reading his script. Mind you, perhaps I could learn more from the man who wrote it. Well, adapted it. Every writer's a robber, all right. Every bard's a bandit. Every poet's a pirate.

'Every poet's a pirate,' I remarked.

'What?'

'Uh, sure, man. I'll see you about eight, then? Looking forward to it.'

'Then look halfway pleased about it. It's a writer's job to frown, not an actor's.'

'Ha! You *do*! By the way, how did I do, y'know, once we got over that Harris trying to strangle me thing?'

Mac looked me in the eye and deepened his frown; jokingly, I think.

)

Early that evening, I made my way along the Royal Mile, which was neither consistently one mile long (the length of a Scots mile varies from place to place and the measurement was in any

68

case abolished) nor consistently Royal (the United Kingdom being neither a kingdom nor united). I had an hour to kill before I went to Mac's – not enough time to justify going all the way home and back. I thought I'd mosey on up to the library on George IV Bridge and study the script. Because I was walking so slowly I was delighted to shadow a crazy old woman whom I hadn't seen for a few years and had presumed dead. I'd last seen her in second year, I think, but I used to see her quite often drifting around the city centre.

She intrigued me. Her hair was grey and white, thin strands matted to thinner strands, and she always wore a filthy blue checked fleece jacket and greyish-black jeans, no matter how warm it was. Her favoured Eau de Cologne was called – well, I don't know the French for Untreated Sewage. She wasn't home-less – or, if she was, she never carried a bag or dragged a trolley behind her all the times I saw her. The only thing she always carried was a toy laser gun – merchandise, no doubt, for some science-fiction film or TV series.

Every so often she would stop in her tracks and fire the laser gun at people in the street: kids, adults, friendly or scowling, it made no difference. Once she locked someone in her sights, she fired. The laser gun had no beam, so firing consisted of pointing it and making a '*Chew-chew-chew*' sound. People's reactions were great. Some people – sour-faced men in suits, grannies struggling with their shopping, daydream-faced kids – used to liven up, shape their fingers into a gun and fire back, noises and all. '*Chew-chew-chew*.'

That was it. Just a harmless drama on the city streets. A little laser gun encounter and everyone went on with their lives.

Some people might look scared, some might turn away; once I saw a young woman run away in horror.

To many the old woman became invisible.

Then, I suppose most of her life was invisible to most people. What was her story? Her name? I had never heard her speak to anyone, just that *'Chew-chew-chew'*. Had she always been this way? Where did she go at night?

I was following her, as close as her fragrance would allow, when, just as I was hirpling by the High Court, I glanced to the other side of the road and saw, approaching the Heart of Midlothian, Mac and Juliette. I stopped tailing the laser gun woman. The Heart of Midlothian is a heart-shaped mosaic built into the street cobbles. It marks the Old Tolbooth, where criminals and doubtless many innocents were executed in front of a bemused public. There are a number of local traditions associated with the heart. One is that if you walk over the heart you will never find true love. Another that if you're a visitor and you spit on the heart you will one day return to Edinburgh. The last is the belief that if a person living in Edinburgh spits on the mosaic heart, they will find true love. It's pretty disgusting.

Mac and Juliette walked together – close, comfortable, natural in each other's company like old friends or . . . I paused, squinted to get a better look. Surely there couldn't be anything more than friendship between them? Then again, what friendship actually meant these days was open to interpretation: soulmates, randoms thrown together, lovebuddies, intimate Platonics, users of each other, enemies; you couldn't keep up with friendship these days.

Ah, good. It looked like they were arguing. I grinned. Mac was shrugging his shoulders. Juliette placed a hand on his arm, as if placating him or asking him to reconsider. He shrugged one more time and her hand fell back to her side.

I nodded to myself. A strange thing, though; as they crossed the Heart of Midlothian, Juliette turned and spat a gob of phlegm into the heart. I winced.

Maybe that spit was aimed, romantically, at me.

I stopped, contemplative, and let them on their way. If that phlegm was meant for me, it was not so much disgusting as beautiful, a kind of deep, romantic kiss in public. Or like kissing me and Edinburgh at the same time. I could live with that.

I crossed the street so that I, too, could spit on the Heart of Midlothian, hopefully before anyone else got there, so our saliva could once again combine, literally and symbolically, on the streets of this amorous, almost fairytale city.

)

The door swung open – 'Hey, Rob' – and I nodded and shuffled past Mac into his flat. My legs were feeling the pain of being used like proper working legs all day, when it was clear to me they were really a wee bit broken. Not broken as in broken, just broken as in . . . not fixed.

'These bones ain't made for walking,' I said and regretted it.

He said, with some actual concern, 'I thought you said you were getting on okay?'

I hobbled to the living room. 'Yeah, it's just . . . I'll be fine in a day or two. I, uh . . . Everything's getting on top of me and what the fuck is it with that Woo–'

I clamped my mouth shut just in time as I clocked, sitting there on the comfy chair – Woolfe.

'. . . That wo . . . man. Uh, hey.' I tried to sound cheery but sounded like a bad actor pretending to be cheery. (Mental note: this is bad, this not being a good actor. Mental note number two: I am a damned good actor.)

'Hey, Rob,' he said, putting a *Brawth* CD to one side. He smiled and stood up and shook my hand (cold, unsure) in his (warm, confident. But not hairy).

I sat down, unzipping my jacket, wondering what this was about.

Was Mac somehow insulting me? He was a friend, inscrutable, yes, but solid. Principled. And yet – unpredictable. What a bastard.

'Rob, Woolfe. Woolfe, Rob.'

'I think we know each other, Mac-man,' said Woolfe.

'Aye, but – *do* you?'

'Still speaking enigmas,' I said.

'Rob is a talented actor. A professional bullshitter, but art is the lie that tells the greater truth and all that, yes?'

We both nodded.

Mac continued. 'And Woolfe is a talented actor. A man with a major career already opening up, yes?'

Woolfe nodded.

I felt a little uncomfortable. The walls were swaying ever so slightly. It was stuffy in here, like the windows had never been opened.

'The thing is,' said Mac, 'I hate it when people bring strangers together and say, I know you guys are going to be the best of friends, you have so much in common, blah blah yadda yadda. Because, like, there's a chance it's the very fact they have so much in common that will polarise them.

'Hemingway and Kawabata both did gentle and violent when they felt the need. When it was appropriate. Listen, sensitivity itself can brutalise. So you see, what I'm getting at is this . . .'

Woolfe and I leaned forwards.

Mac paused. Milking the drama, like a real actor. He made to speak, then sucked his breath in, raised a hand and with casual intensity stroked his chin. He did this for about a minute. Thinks he's Harold Pinter. Still, the guy could have been a decent actor. I almost applauded. He held the silence for a few more moments. Then he floored me: 'I don't care what the hell Paul says. There is one person and one person only in this room who is ideal to be Jekyll and Hyde.'

A deep, pressurised moment like we had suddenly awoken on a submarine. Woolfe and I looked at each other, each sizing the other up in the unguarded moment between actorly cool eyeblinks.

We waited for more; both of us, I am sure, confused. I wondered what Mac was trying to do. Then I realised that since Woolfe knew I'd been acquainted with Mac longer than he had, in the wolf-mind I was surely the better candidate. Then again, writers being so contrary . . . Who knew?

And what if Mac had designs on Juliette? He knew her before I did.

My brain swirled.

Plus what did it mean if Mac did have a preference? How much sway did he have with Paul? I never got the impression they were very close, but Mac was a discreet and unreadable poet and bastard – his poetry was particularly unreadable – and Paul the Jewel a passive-aggressive two-faced hypocrite.

I should be able to work this out. Master that I am of disguises and lies and little manipulations. Think of all I've achieved at and since college. Lies so overwhelming they full-circle, 360, pure as truth. Telling trustworthy and cynical people that you are someone entirely alien to the person you've always been. Persuading them so easily that they don't realise they've been persuaded of anything.

Becoming others.

Best thing for the moment was to be silent and unreadable. I couldn't think of what to say. My head was pounding. I needed fresh air.

Silent and unreadable, I looked at Woolfe, who was silent and
. . . smiling wryly at Mac.

I did not like that. I was dizzy with confusion. The room
began spinning in gentle circles.

I tried to think of something clever to say. I failed. Except, I
didn't; I gave a grim smile, made my excuses and left, leaving an
aura of enigma about my silent unpredictability. I couldn't stand
to be in their claustrophobic company any longer. Who the hell
did they think they were?

Neither of them was the actor I was.

)

After leaving Mac's place I wobbled along through the quiet
hazy streets, turning now and then to see if a taxi had somehow
emerged in silence from the fog. The golden haze of the street-
lights seemed to speak of comfort in the disquieting night,
consoling like lighthouses, halos beaconing out of the night's
immensity.

Time passed swiftly and through the bandaging I heard a
recurrent whooshing sound; it made me feel like I was taking a
meandering path beside a fast dark river. Probably just bats
flurrying through the mist.

I walked for so long without any sign of a taxi that the pain in
my feet yielded to a background pins-and-needles-like numbness. Ticklish rather than sore. The fog and the lack of traffic
and the large solid beautiful Edinburgh buildings made me feel
like I was on a film set and I wondered, with a swift pang of
murderous jealousy, whether or not Woolfe was really destined
to become a film star. I then wondered if the word 'destined'
had any real-life meaning. I looked up reflexively at the stars,
and saw only a huge grey cotton-wool of nothingness. The

thickness of the mist made me gasp. You wanted to reach out and tear it in shreds like so much fibre. It was like a huge ghost blanket, not quite tangible, but there, draining the colour and distance out of life.

Eventually a plan emerged from that fog.

Since all the taxis in Scotland had apparently gone on strike and because I was in the Southside I decided to call at Juliette's flat. She lived nearby in an old tenement on a quiet side-street.

I buzzed her flat from the intercom.

'Hel-lo!' she exclaimed, her voice bursting with energy. I almost felt her breath through the speaker. I suppose she'd found the rehearsals less demanding than I had; I was exhausted.

'Hey there.'

A pause. During which she adopted a new voice, one that was mildly soured with disappointment. 'Rob? What you doing here?'

'Yeah. Rob.'

More silence. I'm measuring out my life in confused moments and awkward pauses.

'Well, can I come in?'

Juliette came to meet me at the security door wearing a red tight-as-clingfilm dress. Her bobbed hair was alive with gloss like moonlight on sea. Her lipstick was incandescent with kiss-ability. She wore a sweet and spicy perfume. My heart buckled.

'Wow.'

'So. Um. How're you doing?'

'I was fine until –' I made a playful grab at the doorframe to steady myself. 'You look like a film star.'

She smiled a smile that had private as well as public signifi-cance. I concentrated for a second, tuned in to her thinking. Actorial empathy. Right now it seemed to me she was thinking

75

of becoming an actual film star. Glitzy fame-crazy futures reeled by. Interesting.

'Do I not get to come in? I can't find a taxi anywhere. I was at Mac's.'

'Yeah, I –'

She paused. Right on cue a car swished past at the end of the street, a black cab. I groaned inside. Felt like kicking the world. But. I turned back to Juliette. 'Didn't have its light on. My legs are killing me. Hell, *everything's* killing me.' I started hobbling past her.

'Drama queen,' she muttered, but she didn't stop me.

Her living room was a draped-lamp and scented-candlelit jumble of the kitsch and the ethnic. It was as full as an egg. Mismatching chairs, bean-bags, movie posters, DVDs, film magazines, cuddly toys and semi-ironic bric-à-brac. I thought of plopping down into a bean-bag but I guessed getting up from that position later would be too painful. I opted for the old green leather chair, slash-scarred on three sides by its previous owner's cat.

Juliette remained standing, cleared her throat. At last, in a too-bright voice, she said, 'So!'

And just then who swaggered in from the kitchen with a glass of red in each hand but Woolfe. The colour drained out of my face. This wasn't possible.

'Hey, Robster. You following me?'

'How did you –?'

'Oh, I hung out with the Mac-meister for a little while. Strange guy, did he ever tell you about that weird American thing and that even weirder South American thing? Then I jumped a cab here, so Juliette and I could, you know, work.'

I managed a weak smile. Woolfe handed Juliette a red glass and they both sat at opposite ends of the raggedy brown couch with the technicolour Elvis-as-Jesus throw. I had too many things to say. I couldn't think of what to say.

Woolfe spoke first. 'So, how *was* your holiday in Italy?'

Was he asking this to emphasise the fact I'd had a holiday when the others hadn't, or because he wanted to seem the gallant one in Juliette's eyes?

'Oh, it was –' Pictures of Italy slideshowed through my mind. The girl I imagined – an all too vivid hallucination – killing herself in front of me. A guy I really did see getting mouth-to-mouth by the Termini. The Pantheon. The incredible tiramisu. 'It was . . . They have good tiramisu.'

'First time in Rome, right?' Woolfe smiled.

One one thousand, two one thousand, one one thousand, two one thousand . . . I counted myself calm in my head.

Silence.

I resumed. 'Time comes though when you have to get back to normality. Or what passes for normality around these parts.'

Silence.

Juliette coughed.

What the hell. A man could go crazy here. I needed to get a better grasp. I risked voicing it aloud. 'Juliette, have you – have you noticed, since you started getting involved in this production, things have started happening? Like, everything's different, in a strange way?'

Juliette spluttered a little red wine over herself. 'What, you saying that this production's going all *supernatural*? Are we being haunted by the ghost of Jekyll and/or Hyde?'

The absurdity of it rang in the air like laughter.

No, they *were* laughing.

Woolfe then said in a tone that was gentle and patronising, 'Yes. Everything's *different* because you've had something, well . . . something of a near-death experience. I mean, I'm personally amazed at how well you've taken it and – how you've taken everything. You're resilient, man. *Brave*. Most people would be holed up in a twelve-cushion bed getting friends to press the remote for them and drip-feed them seedless grapes. You're a *fighter*, man.'

The bastard. I didn't know how I should appear to take this. Indignant/patronised? Or modest/charmed? I think I may have blushed. No, a flush of anger burned over me. The guy was smart, you had to give him that. I turned over in my mind the options open to me. Juliette and Woolfe sat in silence, looking at me. Why was the onus on me all the time? I needed to form a war plan.

The door buzzer sounded, sharp and sonorous in my delicate head. Juliette got up, leaving Woolfe and I staring across at each other. And him with what looked more and more like – was that – was that a *smirk* on his face?

The click of the door opening . . . closing . . . Juliette brought a wiry silver-bearded Chihuahua-faced man into the room, his eyes glittering as if at some private arrogant joke. He smelled of cigars and cedarwood. He looked rich. He had that cunning sparkle in his eyes you see in someone who gets rich exploiting other people's trust in him. If he was an actor, he'd be typecast as Mafia middle-management.

Woolfe grinned, raised his glass and winked at the self-satisfied lapdog. The Chihuahua nodded, his private joke deepening.

'Freddy, this is Robert Lewis, also in the cast. Rob, this is Freddy East-Fortune.'

'. . .'

Juliette glared at me. 'The pre-eminent theatrical agent.'

'Oh. Delighted –'

'Yeah, he's Woolfe's agent, among many other greats.'

I gave my best fake smile. 'The honour is –'

'Actually, Freddy,' said Juliette in a high deferential voice that didn't sound like her, 'before you settle, could you be a hero and get your chauffeur to give Rob a quick lift home? Then we can get down to things. That's good, isn't it, Rob? Save you phoning for a taxi.'

I gritted my teeth, moved my head up and down, the very blood within me seething and writhing, sending tiny spotlights flashing in front of my eyes.

)

I lay on my couch at home and watched my darkened flat quiver behind fat wobbly teardrops. I closed my eyes, let two tears slide hot and salty down my cheeks. I didn't want to go to bed. My bedsheets writhed with invisible little insects. You couldn't see them. They bit you in the middle of the night. When you woke, they stopped. Quantum dust-mites; you look at them, they disappear.

I hated going to bed. In the Italian hotel that night I closed my eyes and screamed a scream that wouldn't come out and when I opened my eyes that room was blood-free and there was no woman's body lying there losing blood and body heat. There was no blood. Nothing. That's how I remembered it, the aftermath.

She stabbed herself in the heart. And yet, it didn't happen. The problem with sleeping is that resting can be the most uncomfortable thing for your mind.

So, I often hate sleeping. It frightens me. I have a recurring dream. A group of adults is gathered in a dim living room. I'm a child. The details of the room are fuzzy; it's almost bare, basic as a lazy set-designer's model. Darkness is beginning to settle outside, blackness encroaching on the window-panes. The room is still and very quiet, as though no one is breathing. Sometimes it's not a living room but a waiting room at a train station and no train ever comes. The people are the same, from what I can make out. There is a woman in one chair, a man in another, and a couple on a couch. They're all middle-aged and silent. The woman beside the man lights a cigarette, her match has the tiniest imaginable halo of light. I think they're my family, my proper family I never knew, the people who could have shaped me, but I'm not sure they like me.

Their faces grow shadowy in the fading light. It's as if the darkness is rubbing them out. Do they want darkness? The man beside the woman lights a cigarette. He inhales and sighs. At a flick of his finger snap! the match fizzles dead and thin cancerous smoke uplifts itself heavenwards. The deep and watchful part of me is scared because this increasingly present sense of absence is as unhealthy and inevitable as hunger. The adult faces succumb to the vindictive gloom. They don't fight it. No one looks happy. The darkness has become part of them. But they were once children like me. They had fun and energy and games and cartoons; they had smiles on their faces. Now, they are fading. And this will happen to me. A gravelly male voice speaks out of the gloom, in Russian, and somehow I understand what it says: 'We are born under a blue sky but we die in a dark forest.' Just then the darkness itself raises what seems a shadowed hand to punish me and instead it sends a batwing swooping towards my face – and my heart batters itself into deeper panic and I wake up in the darkness, a sheen of sweat oiling my skin, my quivering hand stretched towards the bedside lamp.

I made the mistake of sharing this nightmare with The Shrivel. He forced me to attend a course on lucid dreaming on the pretence that it would help with my acting; the idea was, you learned how to embrace the shadow side of your imagination and in setting it free, you became unburdened. Your dreams became lighter and more pleasant and indeed life itself grew joyous, like a happy dream or some bullcrap. I went because I expected to learn how to further extend my range of emotions, harness those joyous emotions for which we Scots are so uncelebrated.

Whenever I got the impression I was going to have a bad dream, I put the ideas into practice. It was much like method acting; it was method imagining. So, now, screwing my eyes tighter, I pictured myself on stage delivering a monologue.

No, wait – bring an audience in first.

Yes. Do this properly. How does it feel? Memory, traitorous narrator and bad librarian though s/he is, is an actor's friend. Even lying on the couch I felt nervousness in my heart, thumping against itself. My heart had a mind of its own these days. I always got this way before a performance. Why did they make me sit here just offstage?

I breathed deeper, closed my eyes tighter. Visualise it. Feel it. Where are you?

I shifted in my seat and peeked out from the wings as poetically overdressed people gravitated in to the old wooden, let's say somehundred-seater, hall, hesitant at first, the way arty people can be, then with increasing assurance as their numbers swelled and my confidence plummeted. For a while the hall tingled with that sparkling electricity of whispering, a thrill of bohemian anticipation. A shadow side, deep apprehension, in this case the deep apprehension of being *me*, was now eclipsing my mind.

The excitement faded. My apprehension did not. I understood Paul the Jewel, who was meant to be introducing me, was late, even by his attention-seeking standards.

Aware of a pulse-like pounding in my head, I touched two instinctive fingers, sweat-wrinkled, against my right inner wrist. Experience told me my heartbeat was too strong, too fast. I estimated 140–150 beats per minute. Panic's paranoid metronome. Images of Dali melting under a furious strobe light flashed through my brain. My mind's not right. I'm not myself.

I felt that someone else was observing my pulse. This must be me dissociating my real self – lying on the couch – with my projected self – sitting on a chair in the wings prior to a performance. In both cases, my pulse was too high because in both cases my pulse was the same.

I took a deep breath, looked up with an attempted smile that came out as a grimace. Someone had moved the chair without my noticing. I was now sitting on the same chair but in the middle of the stage. This was hardly fair. Involuntary teleportation.

Sitting on a chair in the middle of a stage might make you feel significant, important even, but make no mistake; you are on trial. Not innocent until proven guilty.

Some faces looked at me with a smile that said, *I have seen your acting and I know you.* Some looked at me with a wry or a wise or a wide smile that said, *I know you and I have discerned your characters' secret impulses.* Some faces looked at me and said, *I came here with my girlfriend. Who the hell are you?*

Among the audience were wannabe actors, up-and-coming actors and writers and directors of every calibre. Seemed a number of the actors had already done fine performances that day. Some looked at me with bored envy, some with jealous disinterest, some looked at me with a profound, human, casual understanding. I tried to tell myself I deserved top billing at this drama festival tonight. I wanted to sit in a quiet safe room, far from the theatre.

Hey, hadn't it begun that way? Fear pushed reality to the backstage area of my mind.

I was frightened and there wasn't a person on earth who knew it.

How I wished everyone in the audience could see me during the painful hours, the tearful hours, the lonely hours; the times I rehearse my roles until my head is in a state of self-induced shellshock, my body aching, my whole world drained. At the point of complete exhaustion the fully engaged actor's default is . . . empty sadness.

But right now I wanted passion.

Be nice to me. I have given this role my everything. I'm not myself.

The hall was gratifyingly full. That's it – concentrate on the positive.

But amid all their chat and occasional false braying artistic laughter the people out there cast glances that said: *The time is coming when you will have to prove yourself. We are calm and powerful in our safe chairs, but time is battering your nerves like an amphetamined pulse.*

My mind seesawed as it dialogued with itself.

People wouldn't be here if they didn't want to be. They paid to be here.

Aye, but some are critics. All are critics.

Calm yourself. You're an accomplished actor. And try to smile more, you look sour-faced when nervousness seizes you.

My face is ugly as punched clay and I look even uglier when I try to smile in public. God, and the tension in my chest, it's too tight –

That's muscular.

It's tachycardia. The heart's a muscle –

You'll get through this like you have hundreds of times before.

I'll maybe get through it, but events like this are leading me to an unjust early grave.

Quit havering! You'll be fine.

I'm a cinema screen and the film's gone missing. I'm a big white empty blank.

I hadn't even seen her enter the hall. And there she was taking a seat, second row from the front. Ah, good – beside an old lady. Juliette looked so lovely. She had tucked her shimmering black hair under a crimson velvet hat. This had the delightful effect of portraying a freshly familiar Juliette, as when in your upwards glance some blue-skied morning a chalky moon makes you silently cry out in delight. Accentuated by her hat, her curvaceous cheekbones were the physical manifestation of sensuality: kissable bliss.

A stunning moon always puts things in perspective.

I sent her, along with an almost cool, almost controlled half-smile, a telepathic message. *I love you, Juliette.* She – ah, small miracles are still miracles – responded by looking up at me and radiating a full-beam smile. She mouthed the words *Good luck.*

This was what I needed. *Thanks*, I mouthed back with an automatic little wink that was not natural to normal-me but maybe I was turning into a super-me.

I knew I would be all right. Juliette's presence – her public acknowledgement of me – buoyed me spectacularly and I began to relax, both in mind and body. The iron band across my chest slackened. I uncrossed my legs, drew a deep calming breath and let my features settle into something of an enigmatic half-smile.

Paul the Jewel appeared through the fire exit and flounced to the back of the hall to see if there were any stragglers. He didn't seem right, somehow. But when did he ever. Were there stragglers? I hardly cared. Let the good people of Edinburgh come, let them stay at home reading their TV guides, let them go ceilidh dancing through the night's ten thousand glittering back streets. I had my complete audience here, and her name was Juliette.

I inhaled her name, felt the turning point of my breath, then exhaled a cloud of invisible love. Yes, I envisioned my love as a shimmering white light that rose into a rounded mist then floated over and settled down on Juliette, spreading about her like a little gift of well-intentioned ecstasy. It felt so wonderful to picture love emanating from my body then moving towards and finally into her own slender perfect being.

My thoughts gave way to the sigh-like sounds of Paul swishing on to the stage. He turned and gave me a nod. His face startled me. I had never seen such a glaze in any living human being's eyes; they shone like a teddy bear's. The audience seemed to me to give a groan or two in tandem with the floor-boards as people realised Paul was in his cups and this might mean one of his agonising digressing speeches. Then again, he looked so sunk in drink, I wondered if he would choose instead to do the ultimate cop-out introduction. He'd better not.

I gave Paul the Jewel a friendly nod and put a hand on his bony shoulder. I whispered, 'I'm in the zone. I'm with The Flow. I'll do a good monologue tonight.'

'Ah, you will-lll, darling,' he said, too loud and slurring. 'As no one elzzz can.' The artificial bonhomie of the self-poisoned.

Something wasn't right, a strange itching at the back of my mind.

Here he was now, though, the great director, with a glass of red in one hand – where the hell did that come from, does he have a butler in the wings? – and effusive gestures revving up in his other hand. He moved behind the lectern – he, the centrifugal voice who disdained microphones – and he said with a rather, indeed pleasingly, horrible croak in his voice: 'Ladies and gentlemen. Please welcome –'

And I knew it instantly. He was giving me the cop-out introduction. The shiftless, indolent, workshy bastard.

'– a man who needs no introduction. Put your hands together, please!' And with this he gestured one indifferent arm in my general direction.

I got to my feet with a wan smile. I stared at Paul so the audience would also focus on his stick-man body leaving the stage like a puppet with half its strings cut; his boozeful movements, half-willed, half-enforced, provoked some outright laughter from an audience that was now coming to regard the pretentious director for what he was – an object of karmic ridicule – as he tried to shimmy away and instead stumbled off the stage, landing sideways on the solid wooden floor with a satisfying thud and a terrific smash as his wine glass exploded. The audience was divided; some jerked in fright, some laughed. He got up and scuttled away out of sight, hands aflutter, signalling a stagehand to clear the shards away.

What are the bandages for wounded pride?

I was riled Paul gave me such an apathetic and hostile introduction in front of Juliette, but boosted by the fact that she was here and if I did a good performance of the monologue I could gain promotion in her internal *Who's Who*, her private rolling credits, from supporting actor to leading man.

As solid calm gleaming shoes walked me to the lectern, the audience applauded with some gusto. Reassuring. Strength-giving.

I cleared my throat. Experience flicked the internal autopilot switch, as I'd feared it wouldn't, even though it always does.

Relaxation? Paul had inadvertently put me at ease while giving me an in-route to the audience's affections.

Breath control? I inhaled and exhaled a few slow silent *Juliette, I love you*s.

Articulation? I took a sip of water with very little hand tremor and spoke with (pretend but no one knew that) confidence.

'Well, thank you so much, it's truly wonderful to be here with you tonight,' – I was addressing Juliette – 'and I'm hoping for a very special evening together. Thank you for coming, you really don't know what it means to me.'

I almost had to restrain myself from announcing, 'Juliette, I'm yours.' Every moment in Juliette's company intensified the vividness of things, transported me to an Earth, a life, almost begun anew. Her power over me was awesome. Humbling. Frightening. While the applause faded, as it always must, I cleared my throat and began. I heard my voice as a disembodied series of wordless thoughts. I was taking acting to a new level. I was floating my thoughts out over the audience and the people out there in the seats with their faces raised towards me were understanding my ideas. My character's ideas. No, my character was me. My ideas.

Maybe some of us have terrible affinity with the unhappy, the broken, the luckless. Those who have lost their potential personhood and consider the loss irretrievable. The pitiless lonely who figure their only chance to be here is to escape here and who therefore alter their body chemistry.

So many people we could help if we weren't so self-involved. So many people failing in the silent clamour of their own minds. So many excuses.

Before finding love, I had this vague love for people, people I didn't know. Oh, I'd fall in love thirty times a day. That was fine; I kind of was thirty different people a day. I loved, for example, that slim young girl in the Japanese T-shirt striding across at the traffic lights. Her freckle-faced ever-smiling friend. The tall punk girl with the sticker-splattered guitar case.

Every seventh person I saw. Sometimes sixth.

And what did they see when they looked at me? A young man with over-intense eyes, eyes that had seen too little and lived too much. I

87

wanted for people – for anyone – to realise there was a depth to me that might be worth exploring. I was an acclaimed actor, more or less, for God's sakes.

Here, the audience make that poetry-sigh a small crowd will make at a reading to show how clever they are. Oh yes, remember that time I did a poetry performance in one of my guises during my student days. Ripe for parody. *Ripe*. Wait – back to this. Yeah, the mood needs to be right. Long pause for tension.

And what?

Say the little miracle happened. Say one of those girls caught my stare, moved towards me and said Hi. *And let's say that* Hi *was neither* Hi, I'm going to pulverise your heart, *nor* Hi, I will use you and then forcibly lose you.

Cassandra was one of these beautiful-seeming girls. She wore a vivid blue dress and on her inner wrist she had a Hokusai wave tattoo that was both endearing and perilously close to trite. Her multi-coloured hair was dragged into a wild ponytail. We got talking in one of those overpriced 'coffee shops' – what happened to cafés? – the actor in me felt compelled to frequent. She sat on the comfy burgundy couch facing me and stared at her gingerbread latte. She spoke as though she already knew me, or as though talking to strangers were the normal thing to do.

'Look at the size of that cup. You could take a bath in that. Like the sceptical investigator of the supernatural says: that's *a medium? Jebus H Motherhugging Christ, you would drown in the large.'*

I looked at her. 'Drowning in a gingerbread latte is not how I'd like to die.'

'It'd be sweet.' She smiled.

I paused. She had the kind of cheekbones I love, the ones that are both edgy and rounded. Kissable cheekbones. Cute dimples. Sparkly blue eyes. 'I love how your eyes match your dress.'

She took the line. '*I always co-ordinate my eyes with whatever I'm wearing that day.*'

She intrigued me. A person you could have a conversation with.

I put on my wistful Bohemian face. 'Do you ever,' I said, 'think of all your friends and how they're going to die?'

'Oh, I know how some of them are going to die. Hands, for example.'

'Hans? German?'

'No, Hands,' – she shimmied her fingers in front of my face – 'on account of he plays guitar like Hendrix. And gropes people a lot. He's going to OD. He's one of those junkies who'll buy any shit on any skank-assed street corner – you know, like, how heroin, it's always mixed with, say, starch, quinine, powdered milk – I mean, the quinine alone can kill you. All that crap settling into his actual brain. Imagine.' She stared at me. 'He'll buy and use that heroin shit but guess what? He'll only drink decaf coffee. Heroin itself is cut with coffee powder, to y'know give it the brown colour and that's not gonna be decaf 'cause decaf's more expensive. Yeah, so he'll only drink decaf and plus he's a vegan. I mean, what the hell?'

I processed what she was saying. I was going to say something about heroin. I knew nothing about heroin. Those Trainspotting-Edinburgh days were long gone. But it wasn't 44b Scotland Street either. Do people always find other ways of not being themselves? I rubbed my chin and said, 'People are interesting. They are who they are and they . . . are who they're not.' I waited a moment, because I was thinking and because I felt calm in her company. I watched her sip at her drink, kitten-like, if a little slurpy.

She looked at me. 'Poor Hands. Half a loser is still a loser. I mean, divide by zero, right? And you,' she said, with a tiny gingerbread moustache at once cute-ifying and ruining her features, 'if drowning in a latte is not your thing, tell me. How are you going to die?'

'Bike crash.'

So. This was our introduction to each other and to a half-life of ever-increasing familiarity.

Talking together, in those early days, we lived and dialogued like we were part of an indie movie. We felt implicated. Mind twins. We knew the script. Heart tingles. Skin thrills. Tongue shocks. All of it implicating.

Was this love? Separate, we were anticipation; together, we were excitement. We understood, without ever saying so, that life lived like this was life as it wanted to be. This was how, and who, we were meant to be.

Yay for us. We were winning.

Against astounding odds.

So.

She quit her bookshop job in Aberdeen and moved to Edinburgh to be closer to me. She signed up with a despotic temp agency, and I went to college every day to rehearse the end-of-the-academic-year play I was in at the time, Betrayal. I acted my heart out . . . Happiness was a surprise, but not a distraction. I noticed interesting dramatic or literary patterns in actual life. Not the tenapenny templates you get in how-to-write-a-play books. Amazing complex patterns. I wanted to write as well as act. Same thing. Bringing characters to life. Telling lies to tell the truth.

We met up every evening and walked to my flat where we would swap anecdotes and relive, with sufficient hyperbole, the events of our day. We'd cook together, watch a DVD, hot-slide into a voracious physical passion.

In time, I came to realise her imperfections. She was manipulative. She told white lies. She was jealous of my bike. Cycling was for scabby-kneed kids. She sometimes smelled bad; she washed her clothes with hindsight rather than diligence.

Pause for gentle ripple of laughter.

She tantrumed frighteningly when she couldn't get her way. She was envious of my (relative) success, though she'd claimed my being an actor was one of the things that first attracted her to me. She didn't like me speaking to other girls (though I hardly ever did, actresses excepted). She told black lies. She was a terrible cook, but I was afraid to say so in case it would lead to one of her outbursts.

She trapped me, she knew she trapped me, she knew in trapping me she was somehow also trapping herself.

Her resentments grew. She became violent. Violent then remorseful. She threatened to leave me. But she didn't leave me. She lost her job one bad-tempered afternoon. She took to using my money, what little I had. She came home drunk very late one night and wouldn't tell me where she'd been or who she'd been with.

And she floored me the following day, when she asked me to marry her.

She'd bought a second-hand ring.

'It's not second-hand,' she said, 'it's second-finger.' She laughed. Her laughter was a derisive snort and this represented what life had come to be. A laugh at a not very clever joke, a laugh that was ugly and grating, a laugh that was over-familiar and contemptuous.

'It doesn't fit,' I said, my voice breaking. I was dumbfounded and alarmed. As she tried to force the ring over my finger, I said again, by way of an answer, 'It doesn't fit.'

Beginning to end, our relationship lasted thirty-six days.

Pause here for audience reaction.

Maybe life, multitudinous ever-moving controversial life, only offers you one person whose company will truly enrich your life, whose personality will never grow stale. I was wondering if my new post-post-Cassandra love were that person to me. My feelings were not absolute, but they were strong, all the stronger because now – now I didn't seem to have her any more.

As for Cassandra and I, ours was a passing intimacy, negligible in the mindbending scope of things, a chance collision of two dust-mites in a bed on a night of movement and small consequence in a tiny city on a massive planet.

As for my new love and I, ours, should it blossom, would not be one of those open-prison relationships in which each diminishing person settles down to a more or less acceptable level of gameshow banality, simmering compromise and background anguish. Or worse, a hostage situation.

Love.

Love need not do that.

There should be a phrase for one-sided love, a phrase that doesn't include the word 'love' because one-sided love is not love. Love takes two, but it breaks one.

For no one . . . no one ever truly loves themselves.

Ripple of applause for bathos. Curtain down.

It snags halfway.

The audience lapped it up. Bravo. Bravissimo. I looked at Juliette, and something like marvel lit up her eyes.

I basked in her happiness. This is it. Shades of light and dark. Nuances. Levity and tears. I was living off the good adrenaline now. My acting style was a juxtaposition – intense meditations on love, death, transience, language itself, plus swift daft jokes, an unexpected manipulation of language, the emotional nakedness to engage people's affections. Hers? I hoped so. For Juliette's affections were worth more to me than those of the rest of the crowd put together. Sounds wrong, but it's right. Such is love.

During the audience's sustained applause, many in the hall also gave the slow, I-get-it-and-it's-right-that-others-see-that-I-get-it nod. I gave the slow, the-actor-gets-it-that-you-get-it-and-he's-sure-he's-not-the-only-one-who-gets-it-that-you-get-it nod.

Even when I was not looking at Juliette I knew every lovely movement of her being; my own mind-body was involved in innumerable private communions with hers.

I could almost picture the vast surge of brilliance in the days to come, the ecstasy of inspiration, the quickening beautiful togetherness, the living love poem we would make, the great lyricism we owed it to life to create, this huge love we, having dreamed it up, would actualise simply by being together.

Our hearts synchronising.

Amazing, what her flesh-and-blood existence did to my mind. Her physical features, her personality . . . would I feel the same way about her if her nose were covered in warts? Be quiet, and enjoy the applause.

So I hoped I'd given a heartfelt and, please God, heart*winning* performance. I was relieved and animated by the sweet despair of lust and fame. I was close to being happy.

I knew that one day I would stand before a grand audience, with Juliette most radiant among the crowd, and I would give a life-changing performance. I knew it as a certainty.

The curtain meanwhile snagged and snagged and wouldn't descend in front of me and a few people in the audience started to titter. I crimsoned. No matter how good an actor, you cannot fight blushes. Nerves got the better of me. I trembled. The audience laughed at my awkwardness and I tried to turn and run but my legs wouldn't obey me, my shaky legs were stuck fast to that vulnerable spot on the stage and I could do nothing but wince as the cold ugly laughter washed over me and got colder and colder . . .

)

As the curtain snagged again and again, my eyes flicked open in the draught. No. Please. Not morning.

Yes. Light streamed in on cold air through the open window. The window I couldn't remember having opened. Was I awake?

I sent my left palm stinging across my cheek. Yes, said my faceslap.

Is it morning?

Yes, said the clock on the mantel.

I sighed. What a natural actor I was, soliloquising in my sleep, a horizontal Hamlet. The Olivier of oblivion.

I got up off the couch, slouched into the kitchen to discover the milk had gone off despite being seven days within its use-by date. Milk carton dates and their dubious optimism. Dairy predestination – as bogus as the Calvinist sort. I lifted the suspiciously light carton of eggs from the fridge to find it was actually a carton of egg. The single lonely ovum had a crack running down its shell and some long-lost piece of kid-wisdom surfaced: Don't eat an egg if it's cracked.

It looked so pitiful in its weird nest I got to thinking solitariness had caused its fracture.

'Sa matter?' I said to the egg as I carried the carton to the bin. 'The loneliness make you crack up?' My voice echoed in the kitchen, giving an air of ennui to the humour I'd aimed for. Actors often talk to themselves. It begins with learning scripts, reading them out loud until they become second nature. Then, when habit overcomes instinct, you become comfortable in the act and you begin talking to yourself more and more. It goes beyond practising lines in public by pretending you're having a conversation on your mobile phone (always embarrassing when, mid-'chat', your phone rings). No, you get to pretending you're in a film and the toaster over there is one of the cameras, the ceiling light, too. Thank God the cameras are rolling so they captured that great line you just improvised. You're important. On your own? Not a bit of it, you can't get a moment to yourself these days. Life is huge. And you're central, you're implicated.

All of it. You. Implicated.

I want to cry.

)

Cowed by the sadness the lone egg had spread throughout the kitchen and by the fact the sink had shrunk to the size of a soup-bowl, I phoned a taxi and, with my stomach guming, headed over to rehearsals. At a café by the theatre the taxi pulled up with a jolt, sending shooting pains through my lower back and ribs. I cursed the driver – who, I swear, drove with his eyes closed (dreaming of what? – a better life? A better Scotland? An afterlife? Is something more likely to come true if you dream it?) – and gave him a thrillingly insulting five-pence tip. I shambled into the café for a bagel, latte and cinnamon Danish. Mac, a coffeeholic, was there in front of me.

'How's the head?'

Damn. It was fine until he mentioned it. 'Was fine until you mentioned it, now it's killing me.'

He gave a weak smile, his eyes glittering, appraising me. 'Well, I won't mention the legs.'

'They're holding up. They're holding *me* up. Good one, no?' I looked for a smile.

'Aye,' he said, meaning, 'No.'

'God knows why actors seek the approval of writers.'

'Because we can make you heroes and legends, we can make you immortal. Or of course give you horrible lives and/or swift mortality. We're your gods.'

'Then hello, atheism.'

I realised Mac had paid for my breakfast too, though he was only having a coffee.

'Thanks, man. Maybe you are a god, since my head wasn't sore till you mentioned it.' But I swiftly pointed and added, 'Cue inscrutable smile,' just as he gave an inscrutable smile.

)

After a tough morning's rehearsal in which Woolfe and I kept a wary distance from each other but he smarmed his way deeper into everyone's pseudo-affections, I caught up with Juliette and rubbed her back warmly. 'Hey, you.'

She gave a half-jump. Tensed up.

'I want to talk to you,' I said.

'Can't.'

'Wai-wait. Let me rephrase. I *need* to talk to you.'

'Rob, not now. I'm busy –'

'Then when?'

She sighed. 'All right. Meet me in Jekyll and Hyde at seven.'

Our pub. Yes!

)

During the afternoon coffee break I stood to one side doing some stretching exercises. My body ached, but I wanted to show off a little, to pretend I was strong and healthy. All any of us did was pretend. We seemed to do most of our acting offstage.

I twisted the upper half of my body around, pushed down the sharp grimace that wanted to breach its way through my features, and noticed the others had already disappeared. With a sigh, I headed towards the corridor and as I pulled the door open I heard two distinctive voices stage-whispering. I let the door's weight swing it almost shut and pressed my ear to the cold centimetre of gap.

'. . . definitely be a mistake,' Woolfe was saying.

Juliette made a noise that was either a sigh or a dry laugh. I closed my eyes so I could hear better. She said, 'Well, he'll find out about things sooner or later. Who's all coming then? Did – did he accept?'

'Who?'

'You know!'

'Who?'

Juliette laughed. 'You big tease.'

'Tell me!'

Juliette's voice grew coquettish. 'Not that he's as sexy as you. Clint Stenton. Who you're soon going to be bigger than.'

What?

'Oh yeah?'

'Yeah.'

A disgusting noise now sullied the air . . . It sounded as if something heavy fell again and again into a pit of slime. Were they – were they kissing?

I couldn't believe it. I *wouldn't* believe it.

Juliette had better taste than this. She had. Past tense. I'm a better man than Woolfe.

The slurping had stopped, and she was talking again. 'Clint Stenton will, like, for real be there tonight?' I could hear the admiration in her voice.

'He sure will.'

'I love you.'

'Mmm.'

That slimy noise again.

A cool fury started to fizzle in my blood. I took a deep breath. I had to take my time, think, make a plan. What I had to do was:

One. Make Juliette mine. Again.

Two. Make the Jekyll and Hyde roles mine. Again.

Which meant:

Three. Get Woolfe out of the way.

I nodded. Okay. The stakes were high, but I couldn't let Woolfe get off with this. He was the root cause of all my problems.

In the nebulousness of my mind a plan took form. I permitted myself a sly smile. Yes, there was a way to do this.

Oh, and while I'm at it:

Four. Meet Clint Stenton or better yet his agent.

)

The hot gloom of the Jekyll & Hyde pub was turbulent with the inane chatter of city-suits and hobohemians. God, people are boring. And how much more so, with drink. The bullshit megaphone.

Life, friends, is suffering. We must occasionally say so.

I set a couple of drinks down on our table – G'n'T for her, OJ for me – and sat opposite. I knew what to do. I had to be like the old me, but with a hint of a brand new me, too.

'So, what is it you *need* to talk to me about?'

'I think I'm losing my mind,' is what I *thought* of saying but didn't. I was in good actorly control of myself.

I wanted to tell her about my monologue, performed within a dream, but performed with aplomb. I couldn't find the words. 'Do you ever talk to your eggs? Wait, that came out wrong. Guess I just need someone to speak to.'

'I know things are – different,' she said. 'I'm trying to – you know, we need to focus on the play. I mean, I reckon the production should be put back a bit. Like, delay the tour. We'll never get it all ready in time. You do know this?'

'I thought it was just me.'

'No, you're hardly slowing things up at all –'

'I meant, I thought it was just me who thought the tour should be rescheduled.'

'Oh. Well. The Jewel says it's,' she set her hands flying about, '"literally not an option". Venues booked, sporrans emptied.'

'You spoke to him about this?'

'Someone had to. I'm genuinely freaking inside. We're going to have to work weekends, and there isn't enough of a budget for that. It always comes down to money.'

'So the actors could be revolting. Talking of which, he could just get rid of Woolfe, I mean it's senseless –'

'Let's change the subject. We don't have to talk shop.'

So we talked for a while about the cyst she thought she had, the stalker her brother was growing obsessive over, what she considered the occasional heterophobia of the theatre; later she gossiped a little about Mac's previous life and I seized my opportunity and said, casually as I could, 'Is there something going on I should know about?'

She stared at her near-empty drink, maddeningly calm.

She looked at me. 'At what point did we revert to the old American South or to Ancient Rome?'

'Nobody's calling you a slave, Juliette. You keep saying I'm a drama queen.'

'Rob, I don't know what's really going on in that head of yours these days. Did that knock on your head make you forget how you treated me before you upped and fucked off to Italy? Possessive, with a capital P, creepy. I don't owe you anything –'

'I know that, I never said you did. I just . . . I mean, we had something.'

'Yes – had. And what we had was a hug or two in the dark after I'd had a drink. You were too full-on. I was starting to get worried. I'm worth better than that.'

'But I can change. I am changing.'

'Oh, what, you're deeply but calmly in love with me now, my every wish is your dearest command and if I command you to leave me alone you'll do just that and your head won't explode.'

'Well –'

'Cause, you know? I *did* like you at the very beginning, but in the end everything happens for a reason. I gave you a chance but you weren't who I thought you were and you blew it. Just remember this, Robert Lewis, with me most people only get one chance.'

I looked at my empty glass. She plucked her phone off the table and said, 'I'm off to the toilet.' She headed towards the wall that is all frustrating bookcase to full-bladdered tourists but to locals is the gateway to lavatorial Nirvana. While she slipped into a bookcase – strange how sexy it is in a camp and vampy Hammer House way, to see a beautiful woman vanish into a bookcase – I grabbed her handbag off the table and rifled through it for her diary. Ah, here. I licked a finger – yuck, I tasted of salt and grime – and sped through the pages until I came to today's date. It read:

Rehears. 9.30–5
Woolfie's party ♥ 8pm 456 Newington Street
CLINT STENTON!!

)

We left after one more drink. We clumsyhugged and she hailed a cab home. She pushed me away before the hug could get interesting and my heart panged with petulance and I refused to get into the taxi. I thought it might look heroic for me to walk away. I was growing wary of taxis.

I watched her cab rumble and shrink and blend into the fog, its rear lights staring back at me like the hate-filled eyes of an impudent kid. I thought of Woolfe. His presence in my life churned my innards to the sourest vomit. I wished he didn't exist. Something had to be done.

I started walking through the cold Edinburgh night, one heel clicking the pavement louder than the other. Hanover Street. What are you about? Emptiness and disappointment. Edinburgh. What are you about? Same answer. Juliette . . .

Change the subject.

I sighed. Maybe my fellow actors and I had never been that close, with Juliette being the exception, but the behaviour of the others was getting to me. The way their whispering hissed to nothingness when I came close. Or how their body language grew more guarded and bristly when I approached – arms crossing, shoulders straightening, smiles tightening.

I wasn't imagining it. Surely.

Was I?

No.

Life had spiralled downwards since Woolfe came on the scene. Or was it when I went to Italy? The crash? There had to be a way to make sense of all this.

Today in rehearsal, everyone's voices had changed when I came up close. Were they talking about me? Plotting to get rid of me? I just went up to them and said, 'Whatcha talking about?' Eyes darted to eyes darted to shoes.

'Oh, um,' said Drew, all stinking of salt and vinegar, 'Harris reckons every baby is born with blue eyes. Every single baby.'

'Course they are,' said Harris.

'That's kittens you're thinking of, Einstein,' said Juliette.

I knew they hadn't been talking about babies and cats. Liars, all of them. The good actors among them and the bad. 'All kittens,' I said, since they were staring at me anyway, 'are born with their eyes shut. I suppose some people are like that their whole lives, never open them, to see what's there and what's not there.' I turned on my aching heel and plodded off, dignity and enigmaticism intact. Screwthelotofthem.

These days I spent half my time behaving regrettably, the other half regretting my behaviour.

These were the thoughts jostling my mind as I limp-strolled through the Meadows, a tree-lined park that was once a loch. There was still a light fog, not too dense by recent standards, though you still couldn't make out the top of Arthur's Seat, that lovely dead volcano on the horizon.

As I meandered through the cool moist air, a young woman out walking her black labrador hesitated as we passed each other. 'Hey, Mister Serious. Were you just gonna walk past? Like you never saw me?'

I moved round to look at her, startled. She had a model's face, with pure blue eyes and vivid red lips. She clamped a sudden hand to her face. 'Oh God, I'm sorry. I, I thought you were someone else. Jesus, I'm mortified.'

Cassandra? She'd changed quite a bit, but – does a person change this much physically in so short a time? Did Cass have a sister? No, it *was* Cassandra.

I opened my mouth. 'No, wait – I *am* someone else.'

She turned and flashed a worried – no, a scared – glance, then stepped up her pace. 'Rab!'

'Tha-that came out wrong,' I called.

The black labrador – Rab? – stared at me, a low snarl vibrating his slavery throat. Just enough growl to paralyse me. After a long moment he backed off a stride or two then turned and bounded off to his owner, who was already fading in the greyness.

)

Later that night I surveyed Woolfe's house. It was a Georgian building in a swell-to-do part of the Southside and it looked solid and friendly and enticing under the moonlight. One of the chimneypots made my heart miss a beat when it flew into the sky; it was just a bat, but my heart took a while to calm down after that. The other chimneypot was a chimneypot.

Wait, bats don't perch on rooftops. The bat wasn't a bat. It was a crow. Had to be.

A number of the large rooms glowed with a festive-like light, and rumblings and laughter leaked out through the opened windows into the cool silvery air. A few men in tuxedos stood outside the back door; they gestured with expansive smoking hands and barked at each other in mocking voices like long-term friends. I hunched down further behind a sweet-scented bush, wincing at a pain that shot through my left leg every time I moved and at a pain that throbbed in my right leg every time I didn't.

Each window was like a TV screen. The actors – and many of them were actors – played their roles with such a lack of subtlety neither dialogue nor subtitles were needed. That tuxedo was leering at that cocktail dress so much the older tuxedo had noticed it; he now moved between them and hustled the cocktail dress away. Over there a group of evening dresses and tuxedos formed a semi-circle round a grey tuxedo; the grey tuxedo's mouth moved through some seasoned ad-libs and mouths surrounding him gushed with laughter. The grey tuxedo was a wealthy producer. The laughing tuxes and dresses were actors.

Come to think of it, all of them were acting.

Hunkered there in my awkwardness I couldn't help feeling, now that I'd got here, I should be anywhere but here. I was better than this. My acting skills were superior to this. I didn't

103

belong here. But then, I didn't belong anywhere. I may as well not belong here as anywhere.

Gatecrashing is something cool kids do.

I am cool.

Wait. I wasn't even dressed for a gathering like this.

Mind you, if I was going to commit later on the act I'd planned, gatecrashing ought to be a doddle. A gatecrasher is just a surprise, an unexpected guest, and surprises are always welcome at parties.

Aye, right.

No. I should just go home. This was madness. There was no way I could do what I had planned – not now, not ever. What kind of a man in his right mind would do this?

I'll get back through that little gate in the archway and once again no one will see me and I'll go home and come up with another plan, a new idea with some chance of success. That way no one gets hurt. What's going wrong in my life is solvable by other means. I'll get something from the doctor to calm my nerves. Maybe some Valium will do me good, calm sunshine for the brain.

I got up, ready for the flash of pain that ripped through my left thigh but in no way prepared for the thick fists that grabbed me by the collar and twisted my jacket so tight my skin yelped.

'Uh . . . W-w-oolfe?'

'What. The. Hell?' Woolfe's features were warped in fury.

'I-I-I . . .' I-I-I had no idea what to say. Where was my actorly cool now? 'Juliette invited me.'

'Yeah, right. What the hell are you doing here? I could do you for trespassing.' (The way he said 'do you' implied physical rather than legal maneouvring.)

'N-no, no. It's all good. See, um, yeah, Juliette wanted me to come and admire your house.'

He gave a hissing laugh and looked into some moonwards middle distance. His face softened. He was handsome when the light slanted down on him that way. Smelled of forest-like cologne. Expensive. I shook my head like a wet dog.

He looked at me with fresh appraisal in his eyes. 'You know what? We can be of mutual benefit. If you're man enough. *Actor* enough. Are you actor enough?'

'Course I am. Course I fucking am.' The nerve of this guy. 'Uh – to do what?'

He let go of my jacket. I felt like my chest had been stung by steroid-enraged wasps.

'Right. It's like this. Clint Stenton – you know – *the* Clint Stenton – is meant to be here tonight. Only he never turned up and,' Woolfe let out a heavy sigh, 'he's not going to turn up now. Half these people are only here to schmooze with him, and the thing is his non-appearance makes me look *bad*. And not in a good way.' Woolfe stared at me.

I nodded.

'I don't like to look bad and I especially don't like to look bad in front of powerful people. So . . .'

'So . . .'

'So, Robert.' He made my name sound tawdry. 'If you do me a favour, I'll –'

'Let me have the roles?'

He spluttered and laughed. 'Oh, sure, and I'll do up your laces and clean your shoes while I'm at it.'

'Then what?'

'I'll tell Juliette I'm not interested in her. I've got a dozen girls in that party right now would throw themselves at me if I give the Woolfe whistle. I'll tell Juliette that she should make a go of it with you. Fair enough? The parts in the play, though, they're

105

mine, just in case I don't get a certain film role. And also to piss you off a little. So no dice there.'

I hesitated. I was confident I could sweeten Juliette. The roles – well, why not? I could still get them. Easy. If I played things right here I could have Juliette *and* the roles. 'What's the catch? I mean, what do I do?'

'Simple – for a man of your abilities. You become Clint Stenton tonight.'

I sprayed a gasp of laughter. 'What? You are taking the piss, Mister Woolfe.'

He glared at me as he wiped his face, but controlled his voice. 'You're about his height. I'll give you some decent clothes. I mean, obviously you'd never get away with it up close.'

I flinched at the veiled not-quite-criticism of my acting skills. Wait, he was right, if only because of my current physical appearance. Or was he? No, I proved at college I can become someone else. I'd done it many times. Literally scores of times I fooled people in real-life situations.

'All you'll do is dress up smart, maybe have a look at a quick YouTube interview or something to get the mannerisms and accent and such right. Then, just, yeah, we'll take you to the mezzanine, the upper staircase and you make a wee speech about what an honour it is to be at your good friend Woolfe's party with such distinguished guests. Sorry you're late because you have a stinking cold or maybe it's flu and you won't be mingling tonight, sadly, because you would hate to spread bugs around such illustrious company. The whole thing takes five minutes max. I save face, you save yourself a beating.'

I shot him a look.

'Kidding,' he said. 'As it were.'

'I don't know . . . I don't think so. No. No way. Stupidest idea I ever heard.'

'No? Then here's the alternative. I tell Juliette I found you out here in the bushes – I took a photo of you here on my mobile ten minutes ago, by the way, you dozy pillock – and I tell her you were spying on her like the weirdass pervert you are and then . . . Right, sorry, Juliette, sorry, Paul, but what we have here is the kind of unstable *stalker* that needs to be reported to the police and removed from the production. Which, by the way, Juliette already half thinks of you as – a stalker.'

'No, she doesn't. You're a liar. And a complete and utter bastard.' I considered some possibilities. Run away right now? Can't run. Fight him? Can't fight. Become Clint Stenton? Can't seriously do that either. 'I see you for what you are, Woolfe.' I ran my fingers through my hair and thought for a minute.

Mostly I thought of the lucid-dream monologue, of how Juliette had looked at me. One of art's universal unwritten rules is that we owe it to ourselves to live a life at the end of which we can say: I took an occasional beautiful risk. I didn't want to go through life missing opportunities. And this deepseated need to have an audience tugged at me. To have one's existence witnessed, as though more solid proof of existence were necessary. Plus it occurred to me that if Juliette has a little crush on Stenton and then she later finds out Stenton was *me* . . . 'You know what, I'll do this just to save Juliette – *and the play* – from you. Bastard.'

He smiled. 'Do it right. You only get one chance.'

I had a pretty good feeling this was going to go bad. Woolfe had tried to clear a way for me to enter unobserved via the kitchen. He whipped out a mobile the size of a credit card. 'Yo, Poole, my man. Can you ask Gullane and his cronies to smoke round the front of the house instead? Well, you could just tell them, I don't know . . . I have plants out back that have asthma or whatever. You'll think of something.'

Poole didn't think of something. He must've taken Woolfe's instructions verbatim. A gangling tuxedoed figure approached the merry band of smokers and said something to them which was greeted with explosive laughter and what sounded like a request to bring out more champagne.

'Okay,' said Woolfe. 'Plan B.'

'Does B stand for bugger this?'

'B stands for be cool and follow me.'

Woolfe scurried along behind the bushes with remarkable agility. As he moved in near silence, melting into the shadows, he seemed part actual wolf, part spy. I shambled along with, I would probably concede, less grace, but with a superior heroism, pained as I was here, here and even *there*.

As we came to the side of the house, the braying of the men out back faded. We approached the shadowy bulk of the side of the house. A throbbing sound reverberated through my feet. Pompous classical music mixed with hip-hop beats? Ugh. But of course.

'All right, so look up there,' said Woolfe.

'It's the side of a house.'

'There, dimwit. The window.'

'I can't see. Oh, hang on, is it like a square blacker bit?'

'Those are called curtains, that's why it's darker. No one's in the room. You jump up there and grab on to the windowsill. It's the third bedroom and – well, I have East-Fortune staying tonight and he's a smoker so I know it's open. And he's not in the room, he's at the party 'cause he wouldn't want to miss Stenton.'

'Oh yeah, I heard he's going to be here.'

'That's the spirit.'

'The spirit of sarcasm. And while we're at it, what magical trampoline do I use to get up there?'

'It's just a little leap, man. A kid could –'

'My fucking legs are still broken.'

'All right, don't be such a drama queen.' Woolfe paused. 'You can't jump at all?'

Some clouds parted around the moon and a little more light bled through, like a smudgy child's torch straining to be a spotlight.

'. . . would work. So c'mon.'

I snapped out of my reverie. Woolfe was bent in front of me, his butt pointing towards me.

'C'mon, man.'

'Uh.'

'Do it.'

'Uh.'

'Jump on.'

'I, uh –'

'Climb on my back.'

'Oh yeah, right.' I was so stupefied at what I thought he'd been inviting me to do, climbing onto my nemesis's shoulders felt fine, almost natural. It was only when I was sitting on his shoulders and he started to straighten his legs, raising me up, that a wave of weirdness swept over me. It was composed of three parts absurd to four parts wrong. The things we do for . . . reasons that escape us at the time. And even more so later.

He was strong. He hoisted me up with no apparent effort. He emasculated me. I was riled. I wanted to stick a finger in his eye, or maybe a knife.

'Grab the sill.'

I couldn't think what sill was short for. 'What's a sill?'

'The windowsill, genius.'

I grappled for the windowsill. So cold it almost felt wet. I took a grip, let my hands take my weight.

'I'll meet you in the room in two minutes. Don't switch the light on, don't touch anything, don't do anything.'

'Yessir. Twat.'

'Hoist yourself up.'

I took more of the strain and it felt as though the sinews in my arms had caught fire. I paddled my legs against the side of the house, which set them on fire too. Jeez. I needed to get back on my bike, lose some weight. Only takes a few days and the muscle starts turning to jelly.

'Quit kicking the house, dipshit, what did it do to you? You'll have everyone out here looking, the racket you're making.'

I pretended the house was his face and gave one extra hard kick; it sent all hell's worth of pain blasting through my foot and up into my groin, but it was worth it as it pissed Woolfe off and gave me the instant of grip I needed to help leverage myself up against the window. I sat part of my right buttock on the cold window ledge, freeing my left hand to reach under the window and push it fully upwards. It moved inch by inch, squeaking as it rose like in some mad theatrical dream.

'Right, I'm there.'

Woolfe, judging by the silence, had already gone. I pushed myself through the window and put a tentative foot towards the floor of the warm, smoke-reeking room.

Soon, the light snapped on, revealing a sumptuous burgundy room and a hateful handsome Woolfe closing the door behind him.

'Good, no one saw me. Anyone see you?'

'Why, yes. Millions of people saw me in this darkened room. What the hell's that?'

'This is your wig.'

'How come you have a wig ready?'

'Never mind that for now. And in the wardrobe over there we'll find a suit like Stenton might wear.'

I glanced down and sighed; my body seemed to deflate under my dark mud-crusted clothes.

'Which films of Stenton's have you seen?'

'Um. *Extra Shot, My Best Friend's Unicorn Tattoo, I am the Grave of All that is Nothing* and *Blood of My Stepfather 4*.'

'He doesn't mention that last one. Okay. We don't have time to watch any chat show appearances or anything like that. They're getting restless through there. What are his distinguishing features?'

I pictured Stenton's character in the cool indie classic *Mug of Cappuccino*. 'He has a drawl. And he walks a bit like an anaesthetised boxer.'

'No, you idiot. That was him in *Esoteric Cowboy*. Right, strip. And listen, he walks more like he has golf clubs down each trouser leg.'

Woolfe started wrenching my jacket off. I shrugged him away. That told him who was boss. I started undressing.

'Stenton speaks in a very clipped manner, RP. He holds himself straight and proud like a good actor does.' Woolfe straightened his back and a look of arrogance smeared his face. He shook his head. 'What the hell college did you go to?'

I paused, my trousers round my ankles. Let him take note of my muscular cyclist's thighs. They might feel all busted up, but they still looked great. Just a little purpled and purple muscles are still muscles. 'I don't have to do this.'

'Yeah, you kind of do.'

Yeah, I kind of did. Bastard.

I grabbed the shimmering black trousers from Woolfe. The material was almost silky. I tried to be blasé, but I couldn't help noticing the label inside them before I whispered them up over my legs. Their softness was comforting like bandages . . .

'Um – what?'

Woolfe looked at me. 'I said, hurry up. This suit cost more than –'

I pulled the rest of the clothing on. He didn't need to add 'you earn in a year'. I resolved once and for all to bump Woolfe off the J&H project.

'Check yourself in the mirror.'

I shook my head. 'Nope. No can do. I'm avoiding mirrors.'

He snorted. 'The fuck? An actor avoiding mirrors? Would it be any use to ask why?'

'It's a long story. But if you want to look at it one way, the whole mirror thing is a cliché in Jekyll and Hyde.'

'Yeah, but –'

'No buts. Not to the method actor.'

Woolfe began preening my bowtie and cufflinks. It felt good, like he was my servant. My lackey. My slave? Too far.

'Oh, do excuse me, Mr Brando, sir,' said Woolfe. 'Method acting – so you'll be mumbling all night.'

I had something on Woolfe here. I smiled. 'You're not into method acting, then?'

'It's ridiculous and just a little bit precious, don't you think? The greatest deception the devils of method acting ever perpetrated was the myth that method acting is anything better than actual acting.'

'Oh, I don't know. In *becoming* a role, there is a certain merit. You wouldn't believe the things I've done for a role . . . The things I *would do*.'

112

'There's two kinds of acting. Convincing and un-. Talking of which, let's see you become Clint Stenton.'

I hesitated. How capable was I? That's it – if you are not confident, *become a confident person* then take on the role. Easy. Especially with an arrogant moviebrat like Clint Stenton. I tilted my head towards the ceiling, raised one side of my lips into a sneer and gave a harsh haughty laugh. 'So funny. Now, do excuse me, I simply must bend Spielberg's ear over a project.'

Woolfe sucked air through his teeth. 'Jesus, you're going to be there in front of them, maybe not face-to-face, but not a million miles away either. Tone it down a bit. And ear is EEY-uh, not EEY-ir.'

I gave him an imperious stare.

I recalled how Juliette seemed to dote on Stenton. Likely it was less infatuation than career self-interest, but the weird notion came to me that to chat up Juliette in the character of Stenton would be a sick *thrill*.

'I say, how long do you propose I spend among these drones?'

'Your wig's a little squint. There. Oh Christ, the less time the better. Maybe ad-lib a four, maximum five, minute speech then get the merciful hell out of Dodge. Now, paper.'

'For what? They might know his handwriting.'

'To prepare the ad-libs, dummy. But good point – no signing any autographs.'

'One hardly needs a scriptwriting hack for an inconsequential oratory before those buffoons. Those are quite the same people, though a generation older, whom we referred to in acting school as *Self-Mythologisers 'R' Us*, simply grown into bigger egos, bigger suits and bigger houses. Every bit as fake as they ever were.'

I was quite enjoying this now. I almost felt like I was acting the pain out of my body, like I was indeed becoming a new

113

person. Not for the first time. Always took me by surprise though. I started to strut around the room. 'How d'you do? Enchanted? What a delight to see you.'

'Okay, walk a little less like you're a stormtrooper. Keep the neck straight, head high.'

I stopped for a moment, bent down.

'But none of this meeting people close up and kissing hands or whatever you're doing.'

'Tying my shoelace.'

'I'll get it.'

'Okay . . . Not so tight, not so tight, damn it . . . Too tight. Do it again.'

'We're going to keep you on the landing, up above the party. You will make a swift and pleasant speech, not forgetting to mention your great buddy Woolfe. Who, by the way, will be standing right by your elbow. Perhaps even touching that elbow. With an almost vice-like grip. So you don't screw this up in any way shape or form, okay?'

I gave him a look. 'Oh, do shut up.'

'Why do I get the feeling you will fuck this up royally?'

'Because, my dear fellow, like many a fledgling actor you understand very little about the true craft and . . . and . . . sullen art that is acting.'

I was really warming to this.

Woolfe took a deep breath. 'We've waited long enough. More than. Are you ready to do this? Seriously.'

I looked down my nose – which hardly seemed swollen now – and flared my nostrils at him. 'One is most prepared for this. Question is, are one's guests prepared for one?'

He groaned. 'I very much doubt it.'

'Then at last we agree on something.'

I pushed ahead of him, marched out the door.

We strode towards the balcony part of the mezzanine level. The house was opulent, all right. My legs no longer hurt. I walked like a normal healthy person. A little rigid, perhaps, but that was in character. *I* was in character. I was Stenton. Woolfe made an effort to guide me, clinging to my elbow as he'd said.

I halted at the landing. Woolfe stopped beside me. I looked down. Quite a few people here – the men blaring and gesticulating in tuxedos, the women shimmering in a blaze of jewellery and suggestive dresses. They were beautiful. These were the beautiful people.

The women were bright and attractive; they were suns around whom middle-aged fat-bellied men orbited in search of some measure of warmth. They made me sick, the men.

Not the women. They made me horny.

They made Stenton horny. Stenton was always horny. And what Stenton wanted, he got. I scanned the room below for Juliette. Couldn't see her, but didn't have time as Woolfe was clapping his hands together.

'Ladies and gentlemen, I do beg your attention. Yes. Thank you. Indeed, the rumour is true. We have a world-class talent in our midst tonight. Clint Stenton – for it is he – ranks as perhaps the quintessential actor of his generation. A global star of both stage and screen, his many honours include two BAFTA nominations and – being here tonight.'

The joke fell flat, all the more so because I cast upon Woolfe a baleful glare. Jesus, I was loving this. What a thrill to humiliate Woolfe in front of his adoring asskissers. In fact, wasn't that Paul the Jewel down there looking up at us – at me – with imploring eyes? Oh, this was too good. Praise be to Saint Larry. I am such a fine actor.

'He has a very busy schedule indeed and could only stop over in Edinburgh tonight if he could keep his visit to our soirée regrettably brief. Especially as he's been rather knocked for six by a nasty flu virus that's going round.'

The assembled luvvies and groupies gave a collective 'Aw'. They sounded just like actors acting, not actors *being*.

'But better a brief Stenton than no Stenton.'

The crowd smiled audibly.

'So with our apologies and I'm quite sure I can count on it, your understanding, Clint' – I winced when he used my first name – 'can actually only stay here for a couple of minutes.'

'Oh, I don't know,' I said in a rich and resonant RP. 'I dare say I could keep the chauffeur waiting just a little longer.'

Woolfe paled, and fought to control a twinge in his upper lip. Interesting. Not such a good actor now. 'Well, perhaps five minutes,' he said through clenched teeth.

'Five?' I turned with an open-armed gesture to the audience below. 'My dear Woolfie, are you to turn me out on the street when I've only just got here? Were you by any chance a Bethlehem innkeeper in a prior life?'

The tuxedos and dresses gave cheers and little whoops. I could almost feel the air fizzing about Woolfe as he struggled to control his temper.

'I'm sure I can stay for, what,' I appealed to the tuxes and skirts, 'an hour or so?'

They gave up a loud cheer.

'Well, I hardly think – with that script you have to learn?'

'Learn? My dear Woolfe-cub, I am an actor. A method actor. To me lines are not lines, they are . . .' I thought for a moment, angling my head to the crystalline chandelier above '. . . guidelines.'

A flurry of applause from below.

'Yes, I do not memorise lines and present them like some old android. I assume the character. I breathe fire into the night. I . . .' I choked as I realised my accent had almost slipped. I swallowed, cleansing my throat: back to polished RP. '. . . I become a character until that character has no more use of me. I am but a shell. My features, they are putty in the hands of the gods. I am the willing puppet of something Almighty!'

A cacophonous flourish of applause broke out, which bought me time to figure where I was going with this.

Where *was* I going with this?

I chanced a glance at Woolfe out of the corner of my left eye. He was staring at me in a calm fury, his mouth a smile that got stuck halfway. I could tell he was imagining me dead. And if not imagining, planning.

Right back at you, Woolfe.

'I am but one of many actors who attempt to pass on performance artistry for mankind from the previous masters, those beloved actors who, mortal though they were, gave a sort of living permanence to the great characters of Literature. We are – yes! – we are agents of reincarnation. Hamlet has died many times over and, Mr Woolfe will agree with me, it is not unknown for actors to die more than once.' Outwardly I chuckled in politeness at my wit, but inside I caught and shooed away the thought that I might be taking this too far. I reined myself in, just a little.

'In this country alone, we are seeing the emergence of new acting talents. Woolfe himself,' I turned and gestured at an unsure Woolfe with a magnanimous hand, 'Mr Woolfe himself has an admirable talent which shall see him ushered away to Hollywood, Bollywood, I forget which, soon – ah, my friend, the sooner the better.'

Woolfe gave a bow, sleaze and insincerity personified.

'And who can forget Robert Lewis?'

The mild confusion that rippled through the room suggested no one could remember him, far less forget him, but I was now what we used to call in college 'on a roll within a role'. 'Yes, Robert Lewis is the one to watch. His command of the – the polarities of the character arc – the character arc of human existence itself, if you will – is something . . . is something . . . is something to behold.'

Some of the guests were stroking their chins, making mental note of the name. What fun this was turning out to be. My luck was finally changing.

I'm nothing if not a gentleman so I decided to mention one last person. 'Then, there is that sublime and beautiful actress, the pride of Scotland, Juliette Pishwanton-Aberlady.'

A gasp of happy commotion at the downstage left corner indicated where Juliette was standing. She had both hands clasped against her mouth, her eyes startled wide. Stunning blue eyes. So happy.

'Yes, I have heard of Juliette's talent and seen it for myself.'

'When?'

The room turned to fear and ice. Not the room – I did. Robert.

I turned on my heel – which was now beginning to throb a little – and looked at Woolfe's ugly face. 'Pardon?'

'When did your, your esteemed self deign to witness a performance by the lovely and remarkable Juliette and the, uh, uh, Robert Lewis?'

I shifted from one sore foot to another sorer foot. It was getting hot in here, sweat was trickling down my forehead. It was the wig, the wig was too hot. Like wearing a scratchy hat indoors. I resisted – just – the urge to reach up under my 'hair' and scratch a tickly droplet away.

'At ...' I paused. My throat was also getting dry. 'I say, what does a chap do to get a glass of champagne around here?'

As the words were leaving my mouth, a figure started ascending the stairs with a glass of fizzing champagne. A beautiful woman –

Juliette. She had so much make-up on she looked as though she were ready for the stage. Looked stunning with it, though. The red dress sparkled from side to side as she made her way up the stairs; the glass travelled as though it were levitating, smooth and unhurried.

As she came closer, I panged a little to notice that she was smiling in a way I had never before seen her smile. As though she could hardly contain her joy. She outfizzed the champagne. As if she were living out an actual dream. This made me happy and depressed. Happy because I had given her this joy, depressed because I hadn't.

'Since you were so kind – much too kind – to me, it was the least I could do.'

I gave a slight bow, my face frozen; a mask of ambiguity.

What should I do? Say? How do I act in this situation?

And then I couldn't resist. As I took the glass from her hand, I bent down and kissed her hand – in a way that left no room for misinterpretation. I placed my lips, soft, on her warm hand and I pressed my lips to her hand as though her hand were lips and her lip-hands received the kiss and all that the kiss meant and I withdrew a few inches, still looking to the floor.

I raised my gaze just as Woolfe was stepping in to lead Juliette over to the side. She was blushing hard and smiling harder. I gave her a little wink. Her expression changed in an almost imperceptible way, impossible to interpret. It was the tiniest flicker of an expression and I hadn't seen it before, which made me conclude it was therefore most likely to be an expression of extreme contentment.

I now addressed the audience again, with glass raised. 'I thank you millionfold for your most charming hospitality. You are a most radiant audience in your, in your tuxedos and those lovely, lovely dresses. Shapely. Would that the world were like this all the time. A stage though it verily is. On which we are merely players. Winners. And.' I looked at Woolfe with my best sincere smile. 'Losers.' The word daggered his heart, his esteem. I could almost see the dagger. Oh, I had wounded him good-style. He grew sick with rage. White. 'Oh, we have our exits and our entrances. For some of us, that exit,' and here I gave Woolfe another smile, 'that exit comes much too soon.'

I bowed to the audience with a flourish. 'Thank you, thank you, thank you.' Their applause was loud and better earned than any of them realised. I lapped it up. This was my greatest role yet. I'm a human chameleon, a method actor who is beyond method and beyond acting. I can fool all the people. Fuck me, I'm great.

Who among them knew what Stenton's handwriting was like? I could get away with a few autographs. Maybe risk another brief liaison with Juliette. A little flirtation. Seducing Juliette while being someone else – yes, that furtive thrill.

As ever, acting was an addiction. Who could bear to go back-stage while fame's spotlight blinked out and turned cold. I wanted to wait about and be adored. For years hence, many of those who'd been here On the Night Itself would surely have words of praise about me, anecdotes, profound comments.

The waves of applause were abating; they had taken their sweet time, though. I stood at the landing ruminating, smiling down at my audience, wondering what I would do now to maximise my popularity. Another party? One at which I might even reveal my real guise, my Great Act?

No. No. I was high on the triumph of being an actor who had all the figurative and literal aspects of success I *myself* deserved. In a way, it would only be right for me to continue in this role whose actuality was my birthright. I was born for this kind of recognition, this adulation. This deep and widespread love.

In the room below, some patio doors opposite swung open in tandem to reveal two huge men in plain black suits, who stepped aside to let an arrogant figure of a man and a little girl step through. A director and his spoiled princess daughter.

I screwed my eyes shut and opened them again. She wore a pink and white evening dress and glittered at the ears, wrists and cleavage, mesmerising with diamonds. Her hair was sculpted by an artist, her face was a picture of beauty and suggestive of wicked-meets-innocent fun. She was not a girl. Her body was so slender as to suggest a girl in her mid-teens, but she was a woman in her late twenties or early thirties.

An ironic smile played across her lips and, as she surveyed the room, it fell into a hush of confusion.

Confusion spread across her face. She looked up at me. She looked round the near-silent room. She looked up at me again.

I swallowed a little saliva, thick like phlegm.

Everyone in the room was waiting for me to address this gir – this woman.

Silence.

Someone coughed, the kind of cough that's deliberate as a signal.

I looked at the man. I knew him from somewhere. His face would have been handsome but it was contorted in a commotion of simultaneous expressions in the most vulgar manner.

Not an actor then. His suit was spangly, muscular through good tailoring, a cut above the rest. He had money; this explained the princess.

The audience was waiting for me to say something. I glanced at Woolfe. His face was inscrutable. Punchable as ever, but inscrutable.

I decided to speak. 'Yes, my friends?'

'Who the hell are you?' American accent. Her? Texan?

'I'm Clint Stenton, madam, who, might one ask, the hell are you?'

'Is this a joke?' Her face grew as conflicted as her partner's.

'I don't know, madam,' I replied. 'Do you hear me laughing?'

Someone coughed; this time a cough of embarrassment.

I began to sweat again. I tugged at my collar and swept a hand through my hair. The damn wig shifted a little. No one, pray to God, noticed.

I tried again. 'Welcome to my party. That was quite a . . . lovely entrance and you do both look most enchanting. Are we to know who you are? Madam?'

Woolfe's voice materialised beside me, clear and ugly and cologned. 'This is the exquisite Liberty Hall.' The name, nice though it was, meant nothing to me but it meant something to the audience at large as 'I told you so's rushed from one side of the room to the other. I felt a little dizzy.

'Liberty Hall,' I announced in a safe neutral voice.

Play it cool. Don't act, don't react, just be.

The blood drained from my face. I tried to speak, but I forgot English. 'And ththath – tht – tht –'

'Yes,' said Woolfe, in his slowest smarmiest voice, savouring the moment. 'You pathetic joke of a human being. You really think any of us fell for your ludicrous acting?' He turned and gestured to the audience who made a hubbub of noises I found difficult to interpret. My jaw was hanging open. I was still trying to remember how to speak.

I had bigger problems than a potentially hostile audience.

I remembered where I'd seen the guy before, a slightly younger version of him at any rate. *Blood of My Stepfather 4*.

☽

My mind whirled. Run away? Act – that is, lie – my way out? Fight or flight? The room's horrified mutterings faded to a tense and expectant silence. They stared at me with the threatened spontaneous evil of which crowds of supposedly decent people are so capable. I had, I confess, seen some nasty, difficult-to-please audiences before, but this was a whole new realm of displeasure.

Woolfe was leering at me, a joyous malevolence trembling at the corners of his mouth. His eyes sparkled with contempt.

Juliette, looking at me with a confused, almost hurt, expression, stepped closer to Woolfe and linked her arm into his. He patted her arm in a condescending protective manner and a rage began to replace the uncertainty inside me.

I looked again at the audience. A new thought stoked the anger within. *Woolfe set this up all along. He knew this would happen. He planned this whole episode.*

My anger began to find direction. It rejuvenated me. The adrenaline it sent coursing through me strengthened both my body and my resolve. The pain in my legs washed away as if by anaesthetic.

'Why – Mr Stenton, Mzz Hall. I was, of course, only joking. I was a mere diversion while we awaited your arrival, your esteemed arrival. You take my acting too seriously. We were all having quite the jape here –'

Clint and Liberty paid me little heed; he was whispering to one of the gorilla-sized men who had led them in. I could tell by the way her brow furrowed she was internally gathering her fury like an animal readying to strike, but she was balancing her natural feelings against the fact we were among civilised company – and a few photographers, I now realised. My career was dying in front of my eyes. A look of cold determination, aloof and restrained, gave her small white face a classical beauty.

The crowd was now shouting up at me. I couldn't make out everything they said, as they began yelling almost at once, encouraging and feeding off each other. Among less delicate language, I heard 'Imposter', 'Reveal yourself', 'Bloody nerve', 'Pathetic joke of a man'.

'Fight' was not looking like a winning option.

The two bodyguards marched through the crowd towards the stairs.

The crowd's shouts turned to cries of 'Get him'. They began clapping their hands in rhythm. 'Get him! Get him! Get him!'

I had become the quarry. Adrenaline raced through me. How drunk were the people here? Had I done anything so bad?

I turned to Woolfe and Juliette to see if they had any clues, any explanations.

'You make me want to be physically sick,' Juliette said and her voice had that mixture of belief and disbelief that is disgust. She reached over and ripped the wig off my head. The audience below cheered her, then hushed a little as people turned to ask who this idiot was.

Paul the Jewel's high wheedling voice rose above the murmuring, 'Oh, I guessed as much. Robert Lewis. He only just tried to tell everyone he was a great actor!'

'Juliette, look, I can explain. It was him.' I pointed at Woolfe.

Her eyes smouldered with rage then with a speed unnatural to any but an actor, those gorgeous blue eyes turned wet and teardrops quivered and ran down the side of her face. Woolfe pulled her to his shoulder and kissed her on the head. 'A likely story, Lewis.' He shook his head at me in pseudo-disappointment. An ugly merriness, spite, still lit his eyes. He was showing off to the crowd below, but I knew what he was about. He would pay for this.

The audience below was bellowing 'Get him!' again, and as I turned the two huge bodyguards grabbed hold of me, one at either side. The audience cheered. Someone shouted, 'Throw him down the stairs.' People laughed. I had become cheap entertainment for drunken toffs. I gave a sharp wriggle, tried to worm out of their grip, but these two heavies clearly had experience in general manhandling and defenestration techniques. Their hold on me was powerful, steroidal, inhuman.

I looked from one cold face to another. 'I can explain. Really, I can, just let me down.'

I twisted my neck as best I could to get a last glimpse of Juliette, but I couldn't get my head round far enough and it only made the Neanderthals tighten their grip on my arms. The muscles in my arms and legs burned in pain. The bodyguards were so big and their grasp so tight they had raised me off the floor. As such, they carried me down the stairs like I was an old shop mannequin destined for the skip; my legs floated a few inches above the stairs and at least didn't hit against them, which saved me some extra pain.

When we reached the ground floor, however, the people whom I had earlier entertained – entranced, even – treated me like I had committed a crime against humanity. Smarmy middle-aged faces, glowing red, spooned out towards me and spat champagne insults at me. Tanned bejewelled fingers pinched my arms and thick fists punched at my back as I floated past in the middle of my two-man cage. Wealthy nobodies heaped scorn upon me; they laughed, they called me a prick, a loser, a wanker.

(I also heard at least a couple of people saying, in a self-reprimanding tone, that they hadn't quite recognised Cliberty, as the Clint–Liberty celebrity entity was known, either.)

I kept my face inexpressive. Behind my stony mask, wild schemes brewed. Plans that would bring me happy vengeance. These morons' hatred of me was meaningless. Snobs. Spoiled arrogant egotists. They and their opinions could take a flying fuck. They had humiliated me and they would pay. Beginning with Woolfe. The goons carried me through that playground of arm-pinchings and name-callings for what seemed twenty minutes but can scarcely have been two. They came to a halt at the other side of the room. Right in front of –

Clint and – I couldn't remember her name.

She sucked her cheeks in and chewed on them as her eyes locked into mine. I looked down and stared at the shapes her slim thighs made against the tight dress.

'Well?'

I couldn't think of what to say.

Some upper-class yob from behind me said, 'Inform the police. He can be prosecuted for impersonation.'

'I am an actor, for fuck's sake,' I snapped before I could stop myself.

'Oh, you're an actor, are you?' Liberty said – that was her name, Liberty Hall, I thought, with a slight nod. She gave a coquettish little moue. She was milking this like a farmhand. I wouldn't be surprised if she were an actor, too.

Clint was shaking his head slowly from side to side. Patronising git. 'Well, well, well,' he said. 'An actor? We'll just have to take your word for that. Do you hate your "acting" career so much you decided tonight would be a good night to end it? Because, you know, after tonight you won't be able to get so much as an unpaid voice-over on local radio.'

Liberty reached a slender finger out, put it under my chin and lifted my head up, forcing me to meet her gaze. 'I have never in my life been so affronted. You look *nothing like* my husband.'

Those gathered round us laughed and raised their drinks.

'Thank Christ,' said Clint to a round of renewed laughter, more obsequious than ever.

'What in the world *possessed* you, you stupid motherfucker?' Liberty's rage was palpable.

There are times in life when you feel at such a loss you have nothing left to lose. On such occasions, the best remaining option is to salvage some dignity. 'I am an actor! If anything possessed me, the gods of acting did.'

The suits and dresses sniggered.

'Laugh all you want, you rich fucks with your pet gorillas.' The two goons squeezed my arms tighter, as if they were trying to cut the circulation in my arms altogether. I could care less. The adrenaline was back with me. 'Aye. I'm a damn good actor.'

The sniggering grew louder, interspersed with 'You're a genius' and 'Give the man an Oscar.'

I knew how to win my way through this situation. I had been in a position somewhat like this before.

'Think you're all better than me? I'm a better man than you lot any day. Listen. I'm a brilliant actor.'

Their laughter was now bordering on hysteria. What drugs were these people on?

'I can prove it.'

They quietened down a little.

'I fooled all you lot, didn't I? You believed I was Clint Stenton. You believed me. I am. A. Good. Actor. You think therefore I am.'

I puffed my chest out and nodded, fixed my eyes on an imaginary middle-distance, one which saw me on a stage bowing before an overwhelmed crowd, a crowd that was standing up, applauding, stamping their feet –

'You didn't fool *me*. You didn't fool *anyone*.' Clint's expression was serious. Vengeful, even. 'You are an awful actor. These people only humoured you for amusement's sake. You are an embarrassment to yourself and to the noble profession of acting. If you ever cross my path again, or my wife's, it will be the last thing you do as a free man.'

'Well said.'

'Good for you.'

'Bravo.'

I had lost the crowd, again.

For the last time.

The arrogant disdain of these people gave me strength and something to turn that strength against.

'I'm a better actor than you will ever be,' I snarled. 'You don't know the half of it.' My words were submerged in the wild clamouring of the mob.

The tiniest of nods to the gorillas was all the excuse they needed. They tightened their brute grip on my arms still further. Didn't bother me. I had made my mind up about a few things. As they carried me out through the cacophonous demented crowd, I started singing 'Optimist Drowns in Half-filled Bath' to take my mind off the pains I was in and to show the morons I was unfazed, resilient and in all ways a stronger and better human being than any of them were.

I was taken outside through the patio doors. I expected the baying crowds to follow, to witness the end of their ridiculous bloodsport, but it seemed by the muffling of their cheers that the patio doors had closed behind us.

The gorillas dragged me about twenty yards over the lawn and pushed me up against an old crumbly wall. I expected nothing from them more lethal than the stench of their breath and when Gorilla One clenched his hand into a fist, knuckles large as doorknobs, I thought it was no more than a threat. As he pulled that fist back, spitting out a few words about teaching a lesson and manners, I snorted. What did these fuckwits know about manners! I ought to teach them a lesson in irony –

His fist hit me that hard, that fast, I thought someone had launched a cannonball at my stomach. The air exploded from my lungs and I mouthed at thin air, trying to eat some oxygen into the vacuum my insides had become. I gasped for air, thinking, *I'm dying. It wasn't mean to be like this. I got killed by a moron.*

I doubled up as a bat's claw scratched at my head. No, Gorilla One had grabbed hold of my hair and pushed my head down. I wanted to say, *Coward. Pulling hair is cheating.*

'Breathe in through the nose, out through the mouth.'

I couldn't breathe. Staccato chokings attacked my windpipe. One painful teaspoon of air at a time. Little stars sparked in the darkness of the garden and the scent of flowers teased my nostrils. Maybe I could find my way through this, maybe I could breathe. The gorilla kept his hand grasped round my hair, my head forced down. I heard the other gorilla light a cigarette and suck deep on it.

It seemed a long time before my breathing became regular enough that I knew I wouldn't die. I brushed aside the nagging idea that internal bruising can kill you long after an impact. Had the gorilla bruised my internal organs? I felt brittle and rank and bedraggled like something hauled up from the bottom of a loch. I spat up a little blood.

Gorilla One yanked my head up. My torso straightened and I dizzied. Gorilla Two tossed his cigarette butt away, looked at me and shook his head twice. 'Dear, oh dear. What were you thinking?'

A juggernaut fell from the sky. Maybe it was a tank. A plane. Something massive and heavy and unsurvivable smashed down on my head. As my eyes rolled back, I saw a fist rebounding off my skull, but no human fist could hit a person that hard.

The world started sliding like paint down glass, all sounds drowned in an underwater *smmwwwsssssshhhh* and even as time itself slowed down I fell unconscious.

)

A prick of a needle? Something scratched at me. Somebody pinching me tight on the hand. A voice. 'You killed him.'

'I'll kill you in a minute. How many dead people you seen breathing?'

Racking pains in my body subsided. A sickness in my stomach lifted. The grinding in my bones was a comfort, not a soreness. I came to. I came to myself. Renewed.

'At the least you've given him brain damage.'

'He had that already.'

An ecstasy of wickedness surged through my veins.

I opened my eyes. Ah yes, the gorillas. They were hunched over me. I stretched my hands, delighted at how new the simplest of sensations felt. As I reached out, the gorillas jolted backwards.

'Told you he was alive.'

'Yeah, but look at him.'

I gazed back at the one who'd just spoken, stared at him for a while. Gorilla Two, he was. At last I smiled. He frowned. A sick tingling shuddered through me, a disregard for my own safety. For anyone's safety. My senses hyperintensified. I could hear the vain laughter from the party in the house, hear the heavy breathing of the gorillas. A too-sweet smell of rosebushes intermingled with a faint yet thick stench of sweat and cigarettes and chemical-rich deodorant. I could make out their faces, though the moon had shielded herself behind a cloud.

My body felt light and happy. I sat up, and in one fluid move jumped to my feet. This startled the gorillas and surprised even me. Even during my most intensive acting training I was never a great gymnast. My body now had an acrobat's sureness.

I took stock.

The wind made a gentle moan and the cloud-veiled moon peeked out and shone down with just a hint of her thieved silvered sunlight, enough for me to see the monsters that resided in the thugs' faces. In this shady light, their heads looked like giant babies. So vulnerable. I could blind both these morons in one quick move. I listened – drunken pseudo-laughter, a distant dog yapping, the squeak of twigs underfoot, and what sounded like a flag rumpling in the breeze. The spooked-out hooting of an owl. Night sounds.

That sliver of moonlight altered the way I saw things. The things themselves stayed the same, though they were not the same. *I, too, am like this. I have the power to be what I am and what I am not.*

The darkness deepened and the shaft of moonlight brightened. The air held movement as well as stillness in its quiet vitality. Everything intensified, heightened, became more of what it could be. What I was witnessing – what I was experiencing – was the very substance of the visible world as if for the first time.

131

'You gorillas ever hear this? *Satan isn't a fallen angel, God is a risen devil.*' I spoke with fearlessness, authority. I took a deep breath, swallowed the night air whole, its contemptuous human frailties and its musky darkness. I felt immortal. The bodyguards were staring at me hard, dumbstruck.

'I dare you. Make me show you who I really am,' I said in a voice that was yet wasn't mine, a voice calm with bristling rage. 'Get the hell back inside that house. Now. Or so help me –' I glanced down and saw a large stone on the ground – dislodged from the wall, doubtless. It was almost cube-shaped and very big, about a foot long each side. I knelt down and lifted it up as if it were a pebble. I drew it back, dusty in my hand, over my right shoulder, and hurled it into the night. It sailed the twenty yards or so towards the house, landing with a heavy crunching bounce on the gravel by the door. It slithered to a halt in front of the back door.

The two thugs looked at each other and something passed between them. They turned back gingerly towards the house.

I watched them walk with increasing speed all the way back to the house. They glanced over their shoulders from time to time, fearful and disbelieving.

I stood there, feeling like I had connected with a part of me that was deep and powerful and, somehow, inevitable.

The moon broke through, shone down on me with quiet brilliance.

Early the following morning, I woke up the same me but a new man. My muscles throbbed not with pain but readiness. As I showered, I puffed my chest out and raised my arms, drew a deep breath in through my nostrils as the water streamed over me. I was in a movie, the conquering hero accepting his clan's cheers as he poses under lashings of fake rain. As I towelled myself off, I marvelled at how well carved my muscles seemed. I used to be lean, bordering on skinny, but now . . . *strong*. Not an ounce of fat.

I boiled up some water, made some tar coffee. I drained the cup then threw it at the sink – no point washing it, the sink was now so small the cup wouldn't fit in it. The cup smashed to smithereens. I gave a snort of laughter, made for the cupboard where I stored my road-bike.

It was a clear blue day. I threw my right leg over the bike, placed myself in the narrow saddle and pushed off into the pathetic line of cars crawling along, all defeated and servile. Within a hundred yards I had zipped through the green traffic lights and thrown the bike into its highest gear. The Flow was with me. The Flow was part of me, but I was bigger than it. I reeled in any cyclist in my path, passed them with a sneer, left them panting in my wake. I zoomed right past cars, buses, trucks, vans, motorbikes. I lived in the moment and that moment was: the road in front of me, my hands on the bars and my legs spinning at a high cadence in a huge gear, with the air and the traffic and the streets themselves flowing around me. I was Eddy Merckx, I was Marco Pantani, I was Lance Armstrong. No one, but no one, could beat me. No one would humiliate me. I had every right to be here, on my way – at record speed – to rehearsals I was going to *own*.

Let any of those losers get in my way and they'd see what would happen to them. I cared nothing for them. My concern was being Jekyll. My concern was being Hyde. My concern meant embracing fully what it meant to be *me*.

Let those grinning fuckers take the bad with the good.

I reached the theatre in thirteen minutes. A record.

I grinned as I removed my cycling cap and wiped a thin film of sweat from my brow.

I was unstoppable.

)

I burst into the rehearsal room. First to arrive. Good. Gives me a psychological advantage. Not to mention they won't be expecting me at all. A weaker person may have scuttled away, cowering into obscurity. Not me. Not me.

I sat on the stage, shoulders straight, placed my backpack beside me, looked about the silent room. Its self-assured importance was a comfort. I felt at home in places like this, where I could be other people, and in so doing more fully express myself. The possibilities were intoxicating. Even when I'm alone in this room, it makes me feel implicated in something. I unzipped my bag and pulled out the script and my notebook. I leafed through them with a calm hand, nodding to myself from time to time.

The heavy door at last swung open and Paul the Jewel and Juliette strolled through.

Paul: '. . . laugh or cry.'

Juliette: 'I know, right? I was, like, do I try to call him? What if he tried to top himself?'

Paul: 'He wouldn't – would he?'

Juliette: 'I know *I* would, if I was in that – oh!'

The moment they saw me, they froze. Stunned into speechlessness.

It was beautiful.

For what felt like about half a minute, the three of us held our position, as though we were waiting for a curtain to lower. My face was a mask. Oscar Wilde, was it? 'Give a man a mask and he will reveal himself.' My mask of bemused awed self-belief gazed at their masks of dumbfounded incredulity.

I broke the silence. 'You two all right?'

'Y-yes,' said Paul, and his hands began flustering his cravat as he regained control of his limbs. He walked on shaky legs in my direction, Juliette following by his side. 'I didn't – I mean. Um. You're here?'

'Yes. I'm here. Never been more here. Where's everyone else? We have a play to rehearse.'

'But, um. I mean – after last night –'

'What about it?'

'Y-your career . . . your self-respect.'

'I forgive everyone.'

'No, that's not what –'

The door opened again and in swanked Harris, Drew and Woolfe, all three of them laughing like hooligans.

My smile cut their laughter dead.

It was sublime.

'The fuck are you doing here?' asked Woolfe.

'Rehearsing a play. As per contract. *You?*'

They marched up to Paul and Juliette. Their faces were naked confusion. 'Can you believe this guy?' Woolfe said to Paul.

Paul sighed. 'Robert. You haven't been the same since your accident. Wouldn't you – for God's sake, *please* – like to reconsider your position here?'

'I have. And I'm more certain than ever that I'm right for the parts. You don't know how right I am.'

They looked around at each other. No one knew what to say. I love awkward silences. I used to fear them. I'd get all tongue-tied in the potential animosities silence can suggest; I now realised only insecure people felt that way. You learn to savour silences. All it takes is patient greed.

135

Woolfe broke the silence, snarling, 'This is outrageous –'

'I am right, you know. You can't sack us – me – because of what happened last night.'

Juliette moved towards me and put her hands on my left forearm. 'Rob. Don't you think, maybe . . . Maybe you should go away again? Like, aren't you totally mortified after last night?'

'Not at all. What doesn't kill you . . . It was a valuable learning experience. I'm a better actor – indeed, a better person, because of it. I was only trying to help Mr Woolfe out of a predicament.'

I moved myself forwards, pushed off the stage and let my body land on my feet with a jaunty bounce. A day or so ago that would have crippled me.

'So,' I said, extending a hand to Woolfe, 'I have you to thank for that. Your crazy idea to act as Stenton. Man, one day we're going to look back at this and laugh so hard.'

After a longish pause, he stretched his hand out, and I shook it with a grip so tight it made him wince and blink back a tear.

'Good!' I said with a grin far too cheerful to be authentic. 'Now, let's get underway, shall we. Paul?'

Paul, in a daze, gave a vacant nod.

I could feel the spite emanating from my fellow actors; their eyes gave them away. These people were hardly actors at all.

'All right, children,' Paul said, flapping his birds together. My colleagues were fussing about on stage with ideas of how to block the scene. When Paul raised his voice it became not so much authoritative as wheedling. 'Some calm then, please. Don't make me get out my whistle.'

It was true, he really did have a whistle, and on bad days, when his passive-aggressive control-seeking issues were left unsatisfied, he would use that painful patronising whistle the way a sadistic PE teacher might. Its piercing scream demeaned the actors and therefore inspired a lacklustre performance. I wished he would get his whistle out now and patronise these morons.

Pavlovian actor-cattle, I suppose, don't need to hear the whistle very often till the mere threat of it is enough. Everyone quietened down and took up positions, either on stage or in the front row seats, where their splayed-across-the-chairs body language defaulted to arrogant-nonchalant.

Had Paul been a halfway decent director, he would have long since blocked this scene. Too busy playing the part of director instead of actually being one. That kind of thing makes me sick.

'So, Woolfe, would you like to do the final scene, or, or would Rob –'

'I'll do it,' I said in a loud voice, my feet planted firm on the stage.

Woolfe looked about like someone in an uncertain dream, then shuffled off the stage and in a frowning daze took a seat in the front row.

Paul gave a heavy, sympathy-seeking sigh.

Everyone's attention, though, was on me – his included.

Paul raised a hand. 'Okay, let's do it. And, a-three, a-two, a-one – *magic*.'

He fluttered his hand down through the nothingness of air and sighed again. Most of the air in this room was made up of sighings and exhalations of embittered narcissistic remarks, each more pretentious and egotistical than the last. The thing was not to act, but to be. True acting is not acting at all.

Harris (as my butler Poole) and Drew (as prominent lawyer and repressed furtive wannabe perv Utterson) knocked at the door our never-here props guys still hadn't made yet.

'Who is it?' I asked as a weary impatient edgy Jekyll.

Harris pushed his nose into the air – his one concession to acting as a butler – and remarked, 'It's Utterson, sir.' Utterson was my – Jekyll's – lawyer friend, dreary and loveable.

The sight of Harris's snot-crammed nostrils made me long for the day, and it better come soon, when the slackard stage crew got the props finished. How the hell long does it take to make a door? You just take one out of a doorframe no one uses then put it back later. Jeez. Still, it did me good to hear Harris calling me 'sir'.

Now I, Jekyll, had neither time nor inclination to see Utterson. 'Inform him I can see no one at this moment or any other in the conceivable future.'

Harris gave a little bow. Idiot. Is he still going to bow when the door is there? He's going to ruin this production. 'Very good, sir.'

And I was. I was brilliant in this role. I permitted myself a haughty half-smile.

I turned to my (imagined) concoctions and mixed the salts and liquids which, when compounded, released me from that other, less authentic, self. The potion bubbled and seethed, seductive, a hint of something forbidden to come, something joyful and wayward and free. I raised the invisible glass and drank the potion down.

The liquid sparkled on my tongue with a playfulness, a mischief that was endearing and suggestive of . . . something more, something *other*. It had a warmth that was comforting yet it was sharp with promise. The liquid flowed thick and hot and bittersweet down my throat and, as it spread, enlivening my veins, I felt a lightening effect upon my body and mind. My body grew weightless and strong.

A sound, like a door whishing open, almost caught, but couldn't hold, my attention. For my bones were grinding together with a terrific strength, as if they were competing to pulverise each other. The muscles on my arms and legs pumped themselves into rock-like bulges. My body strained against the clothes in which I stood, towering over the little puppet actors and the weak puppet-master. I had the urge to crack their heads together, to smash all their stupid skulls against each other again and again and again and again until they were mush.

Oh, I knew power. I *was* power. I knew myself in this role, I was conscious of a natural – expected, even – leap of welcome to this role. This was who I was meant to be. This was me, stripped of all masks.

Men and women are more than the disguise that clings to and stifles them. In my awful awesome mind a tinge of pity registered, small and transient like a hand waving from a river torrenting towards a waterfall; it was pity for the masses of humans who never taste this great reverberating potential we all have, the potential that made us, the potential that moves the beautiful cancerous sun and the other hellish sparkling stars.

My father was not the loser who abandoned me when I was a mewling infant. Any human father is but a substitute. Even my old self was not my real father. My real father was this almighty potential. The instinct within us that is dormant and makes fools of us until we awaken it and it awakens us. The potential that transgresses boundaries because limitations are false and human rules are fallible and pathetic. Where are the real heroes, the ones who dare risk everything to be their true brave selves? They are nowhere about this earth.

I alone – I alone am beyond the indifferent to-ings and fro-ings of human godawful beings. They are like insects – pointless, feeble, inconsequential.

And they don't understand *pleasure*. They don't live life. Some patterns of routine, like memes, move through them and in this way a semblance of a life, constrictive and artificial and largely empty, passes along. When that person dies, the pattern goes on to a new host, a variant on the old pattern emerges and no one feels like they are living to the utmost or even to the midway point of satisfaction. They fill their lives with clockwork motives, sadnesses half-repressed, joys that are sipped at rather than devoured with a powerful thirst.

There is suffering in the world, but I need not suffer suffering. I shall have command of it. I shall direct it.

As the phrase 'direct it' filled the room, I realised I had been speaking aloud. Fuck! Yes. At what moment did I start voicing my thoughts? I could not tell. But the faces of everyone in the room – Paul, Enfield, Utterson, Woolfe, Drew and ah, that's who entered when I heard the door – Mac and that snivelling Chihuahua-headed hypocrite, Freddy East-Fortune – their faces were blank with dumbfounded stupidity.

That Mac had spent months working on a script I had, it seemed, discarded, meant nothing to me. I was bigger than this play. Play! What are we – children? I'll teach them a lesson.

A thick silence filled the room. No one moved, no one seemed to breathe. It was pure and still and all attention was on me, like at the climactic scene of a play.

'Is that . . .?' East-Fortune said at last. The way he said it, equal parts disgust and disbelief, implied my name was the end of – and answer to – his question.

Someone – Enfield, I think – coughed.

East-Fortune continued, 'It is, isn't it? The fucker who ruined your party, Woolfe.'

'It's him, all right.' Woolfe made a resigned shrug; he spoke with a confidence he hadn't shown earlier. 'Don't ask me why he's here.'

Paul blushed and looked at the floor.

I looked down on these people. Their roles were so predictable to me.

East-Fortune glared at Paul. 'Do you mean to say, you're actually considering *him* for the parts?'

'Well, there's contractual minutiae we need to –'

'The parts of Jekyll and Hyde?'

The silence bristled.

East-Fortune turned and looked at me on the stage, his body language wearily angled in on itself, shoulders hunched, arms crossed, eyebrows clashing, as if imbued with a long and contemplative disgust, and, directing his voice to Mac, he remarked in a slow monotone, 'Jekyll and Hyde.' He granted me an evil smile and said, 'Tell me, Robert –'

I arched an eyebrow.

His malicious leer and a subtle sick thrill in the change of atmosphere were enough to let me – to let all of us – know it. He was about to make The Joke. The Joke that had become to us as real and fearful and hurtful as a scientifically proven curse. Out of that loathsome man's sneering lips spewed an unoriginal piece of derision.

'Yes, tell me. Jekyll and Hyde. Which. One. Are. You. Being. Now?'

There was a moment of horrified silence . . . and obsequious spiteful laughter sprayed from mouths. A hot wave swept over my brain.

141

I howled and leaped off the stage towards Chihuahua-face and in two bounds of my muscular thighs I had grabbed the lapels of his long black coat. I yanked him towards me, close enough for his stinking ratshit breath to cloud my face. His ugly mouth gurned into a mock-smile. I stared deep into his eyes, and Paul and the actors clamoured around me and tried to prise me off the dogfaced charlatan.

'You're not funny,' I whispered. I raised him up off the floor, turned around, gathered all my strength and threw him towards the stage. My strength was phenomenal. I think the others, against their better wishes, were impressed because they gave a gasping sound that was more than surprise; it had a hint of respect.

East-Fortune landed with a *bfrump-crack*, as his body hit the deck and his head the front of the stage. He groaned. My heart swelled with happiness. He raised a shaking hand, touched it to his head and brought it down in front of his face. He looked disappointed not to see blood there. I know I was.

Paul Blinkbonny, half-cowering behind Harris Gorebridge's thick shoulders, said in a faltering voice, 'That's it. Legal reason. You are fired from this production. Never darken our auditorium again.'

'No,' I said, clenching my fists. I made to walk towards him, and as he shrunk away in fright I laughed. 'Coward. You don't fire me. This is not a performance any more. This just got very, very real.'

I scanned the room. Juliette's eyes were narrowed in fear. Hell, so were Harris's. Everyone's. Accessing the authentic me meant I had found a new respect.

I was in charge of things now.

I walked backwards at half-speed towards the seating, watching the others all the time. I turned, paused, picked up my backpack, and swaggered at my own fearless pace towards the door.

A noise. Someone coming after me? I looked round and almost laughed. It was Mac. He looked pathetic striding over towards me. I waited.

When he reached me he hissed, *sotto voce* so the others couldn't hear, 'What the hell did Juliette ever see in you?'

I started walking again, my swagger more pronounced than ever. 'I could say the same about you. I presume you two –'

He walked fast to keep pace with me. 'I mean, you're – well, you're not that good an actor, not compared with Woolfe.'

A fury began spinning like adrenaline through my blood-stream. I was at the mercy of my splintered nerves. And it felt good. 'Have you read your writing? Read it! You're the biggest fucking actor, the biggest fucking fraud around here. You didn't even write *Jekyll and Hyde*.' I yanked the door open and barged into the corridor.

He was still at my heels. 'I'm a better actor than *you*.' His voice was louder now.

'You're a *fake* is what you are.'

He was persistent. 'Neatest trick you ever pulled,' he continued, 'was persuading anyone you were an actor.'

I stopped in my tracks. He halted too.

I appraised Mac. I imagined cuts, bruises and welts appearing on his body. I wanted to damage him. Perhaps crack his ribcage. Or his skull. It struck me that this would be a seeming way to express, in physical manifestation, my hostility towards him. Actual pain. Yes.

I lashed a fist out at his head.

He sidestepped it with a ridiculous ballet-like move and started backing off. 'Violence is for morons,' he said. I made to launch myself at him, and he gave a jump and then ran back down the corridor towards the rehearsal room. I laughed at his cowardice, delighted.

'You writers are all talk,' I yelled after him. 'Words, words, words.'

He dashed into the room, slamming the door shut behind him. I pictured his humiliation in front of the others and smiled.

Maybe I hadn't finalised my plan on what to do next, but I knew it would be something awesome. Something that would bring me still greater redemption. How great life is, when you yield to your deeper instincts, when you release yourself from your cage of 'self', let your fallen angels soar homewards again.

I grew light-headed, my whole spirit dizzy with freedom, and made my way towards the exit, the outside world.

After I unlocked my bike I decided to walk it through the Meadows. People who push their bikes instead of riding them usually annoy me. They take up too much space on the pavement and, worse, they put me in mind of people who can't quite commit themselves to a pet and so find some kind of a surreal alternative.

I strolled down the greenery of Middle Meadow Walk with my bike spinning obediently at my right hand. As I sauntered past the Swedish café, which was fidgeting with chattering students, my thoughts started drifting away, taking me with them.

One image in particular kept breaking through my mind's eye, unwanted and persistent, uncontrollable as television interference. The thing flickered and disappeared a few times, then appeared more solidly and stayed there, keeping ahead of me by a body's length or so. It was a caterpillar. *Look*, I thought to myself with a chuckle, *it's a huge caterpillar leading me on.* So I kept seeing this green caterpillar before me about two metres in length moving along in front of my eyes.

The caterpillar's abdominal segments looked kind of juicy and were fuzzed with hair and the creature moved itself forwards by contracting muscles in its hindmost segments, the ones nearest me, then pushing forward as though its muscles had a domino effect, elongating the torso. The whole motion of the thing grossed me out. There it was. Larger than life.

I looked around. Backpack-carrying students strolled past in voluble pairs, young mums pushed wailing prams, workmen in hi-vis jackets strutted by, cursing the world for what it was or wasn't. No one could see what I could. My new self had hyper-intense visionary powers. So be it.

I watched the caterpillar while I pushed my bike. As the caterpillar proceeded, little wing-pads began to sprout from its body. The wing-pads became clearly defined wings and these wings began to grow. Now there were four very large wings, two at the front and two at the rear. The creature's body had metamorphosed. *I shall call you Kafka*, I thought, *Kafka the Kafkapillar*. Its head was huge now, as was its abdomen. The two were joined by a chest part.

Kafka was no longer a caterpillar. It was a butterfly. How ugly the transformation, and how elegant the result. The butterfly, huge, took off, but as it flew away it seemed at the same time to come closer. It didn't grow any bigger, but I became more and more aware of the mild draught of air its wings blew back into my face.

At last I realised the butterfly was now normal size, centimetres in front of my face. I reached out and cupped it in my left hand.

145

I stopped walking, halting the bike with my right hand and resting its top tube against my upper thigh.

I held the butterfly in my little cage of fingers. Its wings tickled.

I giggled, kissed my absurd hand like a gambler whose life is invested in that handful of dice.

I opened my hand, let – nothingness – let nothingness fly back with an audible whoosh into the nothingness of open air. Invisible and crucial, like a smaller self finding its way home to the larger self.

The Meadows blew soft scented air into my face. I took a deep breath and enjoyed sighing it back out.

I started to saunter down the path again, my bike slinking along by my side. A cat darted across the grass beside me and leapt at a bird. The bird's frantic wings lifted it up, awkward and lopsided, as the cat closed in on it before it regained some control and flew into a branch on a nearby tree.

Single-minded, the cat threw itself at the tree, gave it the briefest tightest hug and scampered up its sides, muscles taut and fluent. At once a paw struck out at the startled bird, and both fell to the ground in a writhing tangle.

She agreed to meet me. My telephoned tears, marvellously conveyed, had convinced her. 'P-please,' I begged, 'th-this is the last time you will ever see me. For old time's sake and in the knowledge, we both know it, that we had good times but will have no new times together, let me say farewell.' Farewell sounds so much more dramatic than goodbye. Maybe that was what clinched it – the anticipation of some drama.

The Camera Obscura seemed a good choice to me; it was a public place, so it wouldn't feed any potential suspicions Juliette harboured, and it was a wise and disorientating place which not only suggested but demonstrated how ambiguous reality is. The simple workings of the camera obscura meld the ghostly magic of a pinhole camera with the bewildering intensity of a periscope; city images reflect down from a high mirror, projecting live pictures of everyday urban mundanities and strangenesses right there in front of you. The mirror tilts and rotates to keep undermining and augmenting what is real. If you hold a piece of paper out, the mirror projects live images from Edinburgh city centre on to the page. Real life on a page. I smiled. You can't help it, as you stand there watching the city which seems so dreamy and toylike, you feel like a deity. I held up a piece of A4 paper on which live scenes from Princes Street played out. Amazing. Right there in front of me, on this sheet of white paper, a little real-life bus drove past a real-life taxi; I scrunched the paper again and again in my gratified hands, imagining the carnage was happening for real. I wish.

No problem. Wish gets.

There was more fun to be had in other rooms and, while I wondered when she would turn up, I went to the Shadow Play exhibit to amuse myself. I watched a young girl performing in front of it, but my loud disgruntled cough and steely glare soon encouraged her to move on to another attraction.

I stood in front of the photo-luminescent wall and bent down into the shape I had adopted after my crash. Shoulders hunched, feet twisted and mangle-angled, arms hanging like an afterthought, head falling towards the ground. That was me, the personification of pathetic. Self-pitying instead of self-seeking. I hated that previous me. I waited for the flash as I'd seen the girl do, then watched the screen; my ugly shadow of a moment ago remained there on the wall. The silhouette was puny and deplorable. I sneered at it, the old me.

Now I stood erect, chest out, back straight, muscles tensed and bulging. The flash exploded.

Standing back, I looked at the superimposed silhouettes. It would be some minutes before they faded. Odd that these two shadows were the same people. Same person. One former and rejected, the other new and burgeoning. Was there a me I was supposed to be? And if so, supposed by whom? Supposed by me, I suppose. The more I filled with hatred for my old self, the more I hungered to find ways to express and develop the new me.

The upright and the hunched me looked like two different people. Or relatives, perhaps – a jaded grandfather and a virile grandson. It was like I was reversing time.

A pang of regret shifted in my heart. It saddened me I had wasted so much of my life being a nobody.

Slow, slow, slow indeed, the silhouettes faded. The old man faded first, like an embarrassment, leaving the strong young silhouette-me standing there like a heroic figure in an epic play.

I decided not to stay and watch that me fade. I turned and left the room and made for the staircase. I buzzed with a happy confidence. The narrow staircase felt powerful under my easy feet.

I caught sight of Juliette a few steps below me. I won't lie – the temptation to push her . . .

'Hey,' she said.

'Hey.'

'Are you okay? You seem –'

'So, look,' I interrupted, 'first I need to say –'

148

'No, you don't need to *say*, you need to *listen*. I'm only here because, unlike you, I'm a good person and I'm willing to give you this one – brief – chance to explain the hell what happened. And *that* is only because I got worried you were going to – do something stupid.'

'Like . . . kill myself?'

'Self-harm, kill yourself. I just don't know – I don't know *you* any more.'

'Mmm.'

'I only have a little time, I have a – an audition. Where's the camera obscura thing?'

'It's upstairs, but to be honest all it is is a dull periscope that makes you a powerless Godzilla and what's the point in that? Auditions for what?'

She looked at her wristwatch. 'Nothing. Freddy is going to film me and send it to a friend in Hollywood, an e-audition. What the hell has been going on?'

'I was wondering that myself for a while, until I figured things out. C'mon, this is where I want to go. For what film?'

'A horror, a deranged professor who's possessed by a former student attacks a sorority party, but it's better than it sounds. Look, what the hell business is it of yours anyway?'

I gestured and led her into the room with the self-multiplying mirrors. You don't even have to touch someone to make them do something. Words, gestures. This I would need to explore further.

'Hey, Juliette, remember when we first started, you know –'

'Rehearsing, yeah.'

'– getting to know each other. I had this idea that, to method act, the, what is it, third-most-filmed and God-knows-how-many-times-staged story ever, I would, you know, avoid the clichés. Like mirrors. People looking into the mirror and then they stare at the reflection so long, doing the soul-searching thing, they forget which one is the real person and which is the image looking out.'

'Oka-aay.' She said it in that drawling manner derived from American dramedy, the 'okay' meaning 'that's not so much okay as weird'. She was not her authentic self. She was mimicking the TV programmes and films her unquestioning mind absorbed like osmosis. She was, in the end, like everyone else. How disappointing.

'Plus, I have always had this thing, like a shrink told me it once. It's because I was fostered by loads of different families, I never settled on any stable identity. I was always tons of different people, even before I took up acting. I mean, which is maybe *why* I took up acting. If you're no one, you're everyone.'

'A shrink? Rob, please listen to me. I've gotta say, will you please, please make an appointment with that shrink?'

'You're missing the point –'

'You do know you need help?'

'You're making me lose my train of thought. Oh yeah, I decided to give this part my everything. I gave myself to it. Opened my whole self up to it.'

'Sure,' she said, though the word seemed hollow. Her voice filled out when she continued. 'I mean we all do, that's what we do, right?'

'I think my mind is a little unhinged. Stand over there.'

'Here? Why?'

'No, to the side a little. Aye, there. And sit down.'

We were sitting opposite each other.

'Unhinged how?'

'I feel weird in a way I've never experienced. Not in a good way.'

'I kinda, like, thought something was going wrong. I'm so glad you've got a shrink to see –'

'Not just with me, though. Ever since that bike crash, the whole world has changed. You've changed. Woolfe has put a sinister spin on everything.'

'Um . . . You can't blame . . .'

'Right, just stay there and keep talking.'

'About what?'

'No, the conversation we're having.'

'Okay. But I think, you know, you're the one who should talk. It helps. To get things out in the open. Oh my dear fucking god.'

'What's wrong?'

'Your face. My . . .'

As we spoke, her face shifted and altered, her nose seemed to melt and blend into a different nose and at the same time her mouth hardened and her beautiful blue eyes grew dark and serious. Quicker than it takes to tell, her face metamorphosed into mine. I turned a knob on the table in front and held it there; our faces were a perfect blend of each other.

'This, too, was myself,' I deadpanned.

'This, too, is freaky fucking shit. How do they do that? It's gross – your face and mine are, like, totally mixed together.'

'Isn't it great! We should have come here before – maybe used some of this technology for the play. Why didn't I think of that ages ago? Or why didn't Paul or the techy guys think of it?'

'They're using whatever that guy did in that old film.'

'Mamoulian. Red lenses, or something. Will that work on stage? Guess it has to. Anyhow, who cares? This is so cool talking to me, who's you, who's us.'

'I don't like it. I'm disorientated.'

'Welcome to my world.'

'Your world is a very confusing place.'

'Yeah –'

'Look, Rob, can we cut all the mind games? Give me back my face.'

I turned the knob.

'And please explain how the hell they do that.'

'It's just mirrors and lights. That's all it takes. See how people can manipulate reality? It's so amazing.'

We stood up and let the next couple – horseyfaced well-bred Home Counties – take their turn. I wondered how much of a difference the trick would make with them. Odd how many couples that stick together are the ones that look like each other.

We wandered round the room, but I kept my eyes to the floor.

'Rob, you said something about feeling unhinged. Can you see how weird things have been for everyone? I want you to get better. Please get professional help. This psychiatrist –'

'I knew it. You want rid of me. Never mind any thought of an *us*.'

'*Us*? That finished before it started –'

'It was just this huge inescapable feeling. My mind felt odd, out of kilter with itself. I had horrible, horrible attacks of despair. Really bad. I don't know why.'

'Aw, Robert, you poor thing. Let me help.' She sounded sincere.

Mind you, so did I. 'I know you'll think I'm wallowing, and that this is because I miss you and you don't miss me, but it's nothing like that. I feel crushed, like everything's wrong. It's truly awful. A mental and a physical feeling. Just *despair*.'

Juliette swallowed what I hoped was a little sob. 'Here.' She reached out a hand to me.

I took it. The warmth of her hand in mine was a comfort and a torture. I wanted more. It reminded me of the good times we had, when we were physically one, on the threshold of intimate inseparability.

I heaved a sigh, brought her hand up to my chin. I bent my head forwards in a manner calculated not to be threatening, nice and slow, and gave her a light kiss, no more than a quick sexless peck on the back of her hand.

'Maybe you're right. Maybe I do need to see that doctor again – the shrink, I mean. Will you – will you help me arrange that?'

'Now? I can't – I mean, yes, yes, of course I will. But, Robert, can we do it, like, later this evening or, if it's okay, tomorrow, even? I have these things to do, they're kind of, well, they're superimportant. Otherwise, you know.'

'I understand. I do. Can you – can you come to my place tonight, whenever you're finished? We'll, I don't know, talk things through and come up with a master plan. I just, I need a friend to support me with this. Feels like what I'm going through is so huge, too huge for one person.'

'Hey, Rob. I'm here for you. I'll swing by yours tonight. We'll get you sorted out, I promise.'

'You're a good person, Juliette.'

She smiled half-voluptuously, mock-punched my chin and withdrew her hand. 'I know, I keep telling you.'

She glanced at her wrist. 'Oh, crap, I've gotta run. Thanks for . . . for being so honest and open and everything. We're getting the old you back again. I'm proud of you.'

She leaned in close, planted a cold sibling-like kiss on my cheek and dashed out the room saying, 'Don't do anything crazy before seven, Robster. It's all coming good.'

I smiled. 'Yes,' I muttered, waving her goodbye. 'It's all coming good, you two-faced bitch.'

As she was leaving, my thoughts stayed with her, following close. Where was she really going? Resentment and jealousy coloured my perception of Juliette these days and I wondered if I was being paranoid or if indeed she were part of the larger conspiracy against me, the one orchestrated either by Woolfe and East-Fortune or by . . . something bigger.

An idea prompted me to action. I rushed down the narrow stairs, past the Escher posters and into a room I'd spotted earlier, one with controllable CCTV cameras we ticket-buyers could play around with. Clever idea. Cater to the voyeur everyone keeps closeted within. On the roof of this building, as with so many in Edinburgh, a couple of cameras surveyed the surroundings. Edinburgh has hundreds and hundreds of CCTV cameras. Everyone knows it. You can't walk down the street or sit on a bus without knowing you're being watched. It changes how a person acts. A lot of people out there are actors without realising it.

Here, though, I had the chance for the first time in my life to control one of these sinister for-your-own-safety cameras. Each camera had two joystick levers like some kind of computer game: one for up, down, left, right, and one for zoom in, zoom out. As I arrived at the booth, a kid who was getting annoyed because he kept getting up and down confused thrust a lever away from him with a huffy hand and a curse and swaggered off to find a parent. I took his place at the rudimentary console and orientated myself with the two joysticks. Getting the hang of it was easy. I zoomed out and turned the surveillance eye on to the Royal Mile.

So, Edinburgh, do you feel safer beneath my watchful eyes?

A sense of power and powerlessness swept over me like a cold sweat. I felt godlike but impotent, surveying my minions. You couldn't help feeling exposed and vulnerable at the way your innocent public self can be scrutinised in such a sly way by strangers. This happens every day of your life. You have no privacy left.

Yes, you do. Where was the CCTV of my bike crash? There was none. Nearby cameras were pointed in other directions. Probably thanks to some CCTV joystick jockey perving up a sexy person sashaying down the street while my body was getting mangled to the left of the screen. The camera only loves violence when it's stylised.

A few minutes later, sure enough, there she was, walking down from the Camera Obscura towards the distinctive crown-spired 900-year-old pseudo-Gothic St Giles' Cathedral, which may be St Giles but is a church not a cathedral. I zoomed in. God, what a smooth swaying curvaceous walk she had . . . Without slowing her pace, she fished a mobile out of her bag and brought it to her ear. Rehearsing lines? I couldn't see her face, couldn't get a better angle, but the fact she slowed her pace, did the mobile phone dance, implied she was talking to someone. I bet it was Woolfe.

Now, why would it be Woolfe? Am I that obsessed? She may be discussing clothes with a girlfriend; she may be discussing Tomas Tranströmer's poetry; she may be discussing what wonderful progress I'm making after my 'incident'. I tweaked the joystick, zoomed in further, following her as she continued down the Royal Mile. At St Giles, right there beside the Heart of Midlothian, she thrust the phone back into her handbag and stood still, waiting. She checked her watch, smoothed her hair. Looked down in, I think, disgust at the Heart of Midlothian. I thought again of my humiliation at Woolfe's party the other night.

What the CCTV screen showed next made me bend in close towards the screen. It looked as though Juliette sent a long trail of saliva splattering down on to the Heart of Midlothian. I had a sorry sensation that she was spitting on my own heart. The heart of mid-loathing.

I stared at her live image there and willed her to turn and look at the camera and smile at me.

She turned and smiled.

She smiled at . . . a figure approaching from . . . I zoomed out. He must have come up the Mound, the artificial hill that connects/separates Edinburgh's New Town and Old Town. Here he was striding towards Juliette like a – like someone in a film. Woolfe?

Hard to see from this angle. He was dressed in a flamboyant long cloak-style jacket, black as all hell. I zoomed in on him. It could be Woolfe's walk. He – the Woolfe-like one – had a hat on – a fedora – so it was impossible to see what colour his hair was. I couldn't be sure it was Woolfe, couldn't be sure it wasn't. Damn.

The couple gave each other a cinematic hug – Woolfe-like lifting Juliette off her feet and holding her close and tight for what must have been an eternity or a full half-minute, and during all that time they kissed like lovers.

I quivered at the console, seething inside. My plans to distribute a little karmic payback strengthened.

When Woolfe-like lowered Juliette back to her feet, they linked arms and began walking towards me. Towards the camera. I zoomed out a little. The fedora hid Woolfe-like's face. It must be him. Who else could it be? They walked like lovers, close, familiar, engaged in each other; even their legs synchronised. A tear-shaped pang moved through my heart, solid-feeling and sad, like a lump in the throat. And then it was gone.

They walked up towards this end of the Royal Mile, but turned to my right, their left, down George IV Bridge and strolled offscreen. The camera would move no further. So, end of that scene, cut to cut to – what? Romantic meal? Seductive drinks, synchronisable legs electrifying each other under the table? Timeless insatiable heavenjuddering bedroom scene?

Someone muttered behind me about hogging the camera and another voice said something about me perving after some couple, to the amusement of a few gurgling dimwits.

I left the Camera Obscura building and went down the Royal Mile, past Deacon Brodie's, the pub named after the eminent conundrum of a man who was by day a cabinetmaker, councillor and businessman and by night a devious burglar. I forced myself to think about him instead of what Juliette and Woolfe-like could be doing.

Brodie found the way to his true self. He used his daytime persona to gain knowledge of his wealthy clients' homes and their routines. He made copies of their keys. Then under the complicit cover of darkness he would steal his way into their homes and help himself to their valuables. He could thus fund his gambling, his mistresses and his illegitimate children. The plebs of all classes couldn't appreciate that this was a human being being human. They hanged him.

With his last breath, he had the last laugh. The gallows upon which they hanged him had recently been redesigned by . . . Brodie himself. He boasted of the gallows' efficiency to those gathered before him, that baying sneering crowd of civilised bloodthirsty Edinburghers. I could imagine myself making a speech like that.

William Brodie was so well respected as a craftsman that Robert Louis Stevenson's well-to-do daddy had him build furniture for the family home, thus inspiring – part-inspiring would be more appropriate – Robert Louis Stevenson's creation, Dr Jekyll/Mr Hyde. Except Stevenson did not create Dr Jekyll/Mr Hyde. He revealed them. Him. Them. He shed the right amount of shadowy light upon that which is within us all.

Thus I mused as I passed Deacon Brodie's pub, which was in the business of altering decent people into their deeper selves by way of sweetened poisons, titillating depressants.

I crossed at the traffic lights, and started moseying up George IV Bridge, avoiding a swarm of lovely Japanese tourists flashing V-fingered peace signs at matchbox-sized cameras. What do they make of this divided city, this nation that isn't? There is no Scotland. No Edinburgh. They exist in the plural. These are places that have not yet found their true and lasting selves.

Don't people see what life really is? Rather, *why* don't they see what life really is?

As I made my way down the street, I thought I saw Juliette stop with Woolfe-like beside a black car some hundred or so yards up the road, opposite that café where JK Rowling ate some cakes and opened a notepad and in so doing multiplied the café's profits millionfold.

Strange, how things interconnect.

Woolfe-like turned, with an arm on Juliette's shoulder, and opened a car door. A sleek black car. 'No,' I pleaded under my breath. Did no good. She crouched and stepped into the car. Woolfe-like closed the door behind her like a sugar daddy or a chauffeur and, with what seemed a glance in my direction, walked round the car, opened the driver's side door and got in. The car started up almost at once and moved, fast and smooth, into the easy traffic.

Damn it. She was mine. Her heart was mine.

No point in following the car – unless . . . Unless I went back to my bike (it wasn't far), jumped in the saddle and pedalled hard. There was no doubt I could keep up with a car in traffic – even in heavy urban traffic. Cycling a road-bike at speeds well in excess of 30 mph is not that hard. You need to be fit, is all, and I've never been stronger.

I'd left my bike chained up at the Swedish café in the Meadows. No harm in walking down there, jumping in the saddle and having a scoot around. I hadn't finished with Juliette yet; I'd hardly even started.

As I crossed the street towards the Meadows, ignoring the lights since there was no traffic, a dark car rocketed towards me. I jumped out of its way just in time. My face flamed into anger when I realised it was the black car Juliette had climbed into. There she was! Her face swivelling to look at me in mock horror at the near-accident. The car had swooshed so close to me I felt it slap the side of my jacket. It slowed down a little, the driver looked into the rearview mirror.

I recognised those duplicitous greedy marbles that glinted back at me. Woolfe's eyes. Now crinkling in laughter lines. There was a third person in the car – it was that vile waste of life, Freddy East-Fortune. The car honked twice in sarcasm and then floored it westwards, towards Lothian Road.

I paused, watching the car speed away. She wasn't *that* great an actress, so it was hard to tell – did her expression suggest a measure of actual fear? Had she fashioned her own unwitting punishment?

I unchained my bike from the railings, slung the heavy lock – cost forty pounds and weighs as much – into my backpack and jumped in the saddle.

I pedalled a couple of easy revolutions up Middle Meadow Walk. The wind was cool in my hair – ah. I forgot to put on my helmet, still in my backpack. No matter.

A girl in a red top I cycled past had me picturing blood spreading across Juliette's chest. Like in the 'Scottish' play I'd once been in. How different real blood would look. Poor Juliette. What kind of horror was she going to be in?

As I cycled up towards the road I couldn't resist upping my cadence a little. Cycling at walking pace felt like a betrayal of human potential. That's it. Swift, the way a road-bike likes to be ridden.

But not *too* swift. My legs enjoyed the circles they described in the air, the bike was alive under me – it was part of me. Some people sat hunched over wine bottles and books, a reading group maybe; some teenagers played a game of football with jackets for goalposts; some tanned athletic types arranged in a hexagon shape threw frisbees at each other. I gave the world a contented sigh. The way I planned to revenge myself on Woolfe and the others gave my heart a little bump of joy.

I turned left at the top of the path and thudded gently off the kerb on to the road, which was humming with random traffic. I took my place among the fourwheelers, good air pressure in my tyres buoying me along, strength in my legs – and plenty reserves of it, too. I was in The Flow, relaxed control in my hands half-clasped on the brakehoods, fingers ready to feather the brake levers if necessary, a lightness in my muscle mass, a definition, a –

close call. As I cycled by Quartermile, where the old Royal Infirmary used to be, I realised the taxi in front of me had come to a stop without indicating. Nowhere near enough distance between me and the taxi to brake without colliding, so I swung out at a supersharp angle into the middle of the road, no other course of action but

but a car was travelling towards me, also bypassing stationary cars, also in the middle of the road. I pulled my readied fingers hard on the brake levers, my wheels locked, and it almost seemed the car headed towards me was speeding up. I eased my grip a little, my wheels unlocked. What the hell? The car was hardly braking, if at all. I yanked on my brakes again, just right, not so tight as to lock the wheels, and the car too fast toofast-toofast smashed likeabomb into my bike. I heard and felt a crack somewhere, my front wheel buckled, the base of my spine crunched, my feet lifted out of the pedals, the bike folded in on itself; at the same time the rear end launched itself skywards, hurling me out of the saddle, I sailed over the handlebars, I was weightless, I flew along the bonnet towards the windscreen and I knew I was going to die. So much unsaid undone, and it seemed to me the look on the driver's face was altogether too calm and the last thing I saw before I hit the windscreen and died was that ugly expressionless face I recognised almost too late, the last face I saw on earth belonged to Mac, and I just prayed my death would also cause his

'We shall find in our troubled hearts, where discord reigns, two needs which seem at variance, but which merge, as I think, in a common source – the love of the true, and the love of the fabulous.'

Alfred de Vigny

PART TWO

That Small Theatre of the Brain, Lighted

Julie's Narrative

'It's not easy being me.'
Almost everyone, much of the time.

There once was a man who died and came back to life the same but changed. Even before he died he was a difficult man to describe and I'm no writer so let's just say . . . He was handsome to some and not so much to others, he was thoughtful, compli-cated, witty, deep, silly, self-destructive, compassionate, intelli-gent, illogical, insecure, thoughtless, narcissistic, self-loathing, gentle, sympathetic, naive, kind-hearted, cynical, depressive and imaginative. Among other things!

To fight the depressions and anxieties that came upon him, he took up an unlikely weapon.

A bicycle.

Not just any bike because, true to his two-sided nature, this man needed a bike that separated him from others but without drawing attention to himself. If it was challenging to ride, so that he could both punish himself and show off, all the better. So he bought a fixed-gear bike, which is more difficult to ride than a geared bike because the bike only moves when you pedal and you can't freewheel to make it easy going downhill and neither can you change gear to make it easier when going uphill.

The bike looked very cool even to someone like me who knows nothing about cycling and, yeah, I reckoned he looked cool on it, whooshing about among the buses and taxis and cars, though this also made me nervous for his safety – still, I didn't want to think about that in case I jinxed him. After quite a few thousand(!) miles of cycling, which included indoor training when the Edinburgh weather got a bit too Scottish, he became what he called a 'competent' cyclist. In fact, he was a very good bike rider indeed, though he didn't usually see it that way because even if in some parallel universe he won an Olympic gold medal he would say, 'I only won it because so-and-so wasn't in top form today.'

One morning while out riding his fixed-gear bike he was involved in a serious accident. What happened is unclear. Either he was cycling too fast on the inside lane, in a blind spot between the kerb and the truck itself, or as I think more likely, the lorry driver didn't check his mirrors before making a sharp hasty turn down a little-used alley, cutting into the bike's path, totally and unfairly blindsiding the rider.

He lost consciousness at the moment of impact, and as far as I can make out he was not responsive to the paramedics who arrived shortly after the accident. I don't know who, if anyone, phoned for the ambulance; there were no witnesses and CCTV cameras failed to pick up the incident despite the fact it happened right next to a police station.

One of the paramedics was himself a cyclist and said he couldn't believe anyone could survive the accident judging by the faintness of the man's pulse and the wreckage of what had been a bike.

I was torn apart. Deep down, I *knew* something like this would happen sooner or later. I wondered if there was anything I could have done. Should I have warned him I heard even professional cyclists can crash and die? Nagged him to give up cycling? That wasn't in my nature.

This is how I heard about it: a friend of a friend sent me a text message informing me that the man – my man – had been seen, or someone like him, getting stretchered into an ambulance, moaning and bleeding profusely, or else lifeless with a white sheet tossed over his face depending on who you believed.

I rang round our little capital city's hospitals and traced the man to the Royal Infirmary. I didn't trust my trembling limbs and scatterflying mind to drive, so I called a taxi and when I reached the hospital I was fortunate enough literally to run into a lifesaver of a woman named Nurse Stevenson, who pretended to believe my lie that I was the man's wife. Different surnames, no wedding rings. Nurse Stevenson was a godsend.

The nurse persuaded me the only possible course of action for the moment was to sit, quiet and patient if I at all could, in a white room with these horrible nicey-nice pastel paintings of flowers and sunrises on the wall and a plain low table with a bunch of stupid celebrity magazines and a box of hankies. Here I could drink regular cups of tea, which were free since there was a kettle, and packets of crisps, which were available from an overpriced vending machine. I ate packet after packet of crisps to give myself something to do and I drank countless cups of tea. This was to become my new diet. I watched a big simple clock grind its hands round in slowmotion circles like it was playing nasty games with me.

All night I sat in that room trying to picture a life without the man. For every fault he harboured, I saw in him a more-than-redeeming flash of goodness. Why else would I have stayed with him? He didn't want to be insecure or self-loathing – these, I knew, were like diseases he would shake off. He didn't choose to suffer depression – that, I knew, was an illness I could help – *was* helping – to cure.

At long long last, just as dawn was lighting its way through the thin curtains, Nurse Stevenson returned and told me that things were touch-and-go for a long time, but not to worry as one thing was for sure, the man was a fighter – 'Even fighting himself at times.' I was all wrung out like a manky old tourniquet, but I marvelled at how fresh and composed this nurse looked after what must have been a long and stressful night. Her

167

skin was clear and unblemished, her eyes calm yet full of sparkle. By contrast, I felt as though my raw sleepless eyes had been scraped and blowtorched by something from a sadistic film. Everything felt unreal. And yet it was real.

Nurse Stevenson was so radiant. What did she radiate? Compassion? Energy? The simple care implicit in a clean uniform? A sense of comfort, of understanding. Meanwhile I had a need. No doubt about it, this was a kind and approachable nurse and asking her was the best option. I cleared my throat, took a breath and spoke, all my words running together. 'IsheokaycanIseehimwillhebeallright?'

Nurse Stevenson sat on the couch beside me and took my hand, sandwiched it between her own. No woman ever held my hand like this. It calmed me to an astonishing degree.

'The doctors thought they'd lost him. More than once. But I,' and the nurse looked deep into my eyes here, 'I have faith he'll get through this.'

'Can I see him? Please? I'm begging you.' I did – I pleaded. I'd never begged for anything before. It should have felt humiliating, but beside – and in the hands of – Nurse Stevenson, it felt honest, natural. No need for trivial anxieties about asking for something. Normally I never opened up to strangers like this. But none of this was normal.

'He's still in ICU. I'm not meant to . . . Well, you won't get me into trouble, I know. Follow me.' When the nurse released my hand and stood up to make for the door, I half-wished I could trail along beside her with my hand in hers.

∪

Nurse Stevenson let me enter the room first. I clasped my hand to my mouth. I thought I had readied myself but . . . He lay there, bandaged about the head and chest, attached to tubes and electronic machines; I could see perfectly well that he was dead.

I was about to cry. I could feel the tears welling in my eyes.

The man began twitching his arms and legs. He was unconscious, but you could see how pain warped his face. He seemed to be dragging his legs up and down, wincing and moving his mouth as though muttering to himself in some silent private language.

I turned, and Nurse Stevenson was standing right beside me. I lay my head on the nurse's shoulder and said, my voice no more than a whisper, 'Can I stay here?'

The nurse stroked my hair. No one other than my boyfriend and my deceased mother and my uncle who didn't count had ever stroked my hair. It soothed me.

'Okay,' said the nurse, 'but if anyone asks, you never saw me. And if any of the machines – especially that one there – change their sound or any alarms or buzzers go off, get out of here, hide.'

I moved towards him with trepidation, paranoid I would damage him in some way or remove one of the tubes or pads connecting him to the complicated technology that seemed to be keeping him alive. I took a very deep breath, gathered myself.

I placed my hand on his and bent forward to kiss him beneath a bandage on his forehead. He smelled of antiseptic and blood and the reek of my own cheese-and-onion breath rebounded back on me. A weird thought-combination of life&death made a morbid jangling in my nerves. I gave him a lingering kiss. My heart sped up, in a good way.

I couldn't speak. Instead, I watched him mouth inaccessible words to himself. I leaned in close to hear what he was trying to say. I couldn't make anything out. If he died and I couldn't understand his final words – no, I wasn't going to allow myself to think like that.

I strained to listen to him for as long as I could, but being up all night with nothing to do but worry and eat crisps and worry and drink tea and worry and go to the toilet and worry and pace about the floor had left my body exhausted, and after a while I fell asleep, leaning on the bed, half-standing, my head beside his on the pillow. I dreamed that I saw him, just for a moment in a strange peaceful place, but when we leaned in to hug I pushed him away.

U

I woke up confused, frowning, wincing at a crick in my neck. A few blinks of my tired eyes and I realised I was staring close up into my boyfriend's twisted face. In hospital. I glanced at my watch. I'd slept for only 20 minutes or so, a micro-sleep, but I felt refreshed enough to stand and stretch.

'Is this your husband?' A male voice behind me made me jump.

'No.' I wheeled round to face a young doctor. 'Yes, I mean he – he just seems so different.'

I gestured towards the man lying in the sterile bed and as the doctor made to speak, the man began jerking around again but this time as if he was having an epileptic fit. I was scared. 'Will he be okay?'

The doctor's whole manner changed. 'I need you out of here – now. Go!' He pushed me towards the door and I stepped through to see a team of men and women hurtling down the corridor with a trolley. I took a stride backwards and the medical staff veered into the room I'd just exited.

My first instinct was to scream and run into the room, my second to dash in and ask if I could help in any way, my third instinct told me none of these was rational so I could either wait in the hospital or go somewhere else. The antiseptic smells and echoey sounds of the hospital were beginning to depress me a little and I reckoned that if my boyfriend was dying right there and then, I did not want to be a few feet away, I did not want to be in the same building. In this way I forced myself to decide to leave and I felt somehow relieved at leaving.

U

In the cool morning I wandered about a changed world. Everything looked the same as it ever did – even the blue sky promised a nice day – but in substance, and for ever, everything had changed. Vehicles moved about in front of me, engines of death, transporting the dying, some dying slowly, some dying quickly, some dying, perhaps, suddenly when that very bus crashed, on a day like this, with a promising blue sky; everything taken away.

Taken where?

Even the sun that was rising in the blue was sending out rays that offered warmth but delivered cancer, like a kindly uncle who took you in his lap and then started telling you there was no God or told you, after crossing his heart and hoping to die, ghost stories that were 'as true as I'm sitting here' and kept you awake at night, clutching the blanket, stiff with fear.

I wanted to scream. The tiredness didn't help.

If my boyfriend was going to die, could I get them to freeze his sperm for me? Why couldn't I be pregnant right now?

Wait, did I really want to be pregnant? No.

But if he was really going to die would I want to be pregnant? I didn't know.

How life changes – in less time than it takes to describe it, a life can be taken away or a decision made that affects everything for ever.

My stomach was growling but I couldn't eat. My body was still tired but no way could I sleep. I was tense and hollow. I would be a good mother. Maybe. Other times I thought of motherhood it scared me and I reckoned I'd be a terrible mother, cranky with sleeplessness and selfish for the little freedoms like choosing to go to the cinema at the last minute so you had to run to get there, panting and exhilarated, just as the main feature was beginning. I didn't know what to do right now, who to call, where to go. I knew almost nothing about his parents – though he was an open book in some ways, in other ways he was deep and reflective and hard to connect with. Almost autistic. I felt bad for thinking that. It wasn't true. The stress was getting to me. I had no idea where that thought had come from and I felt worthless for having thought it at all.

He went to some dark places inside himself, I knew that, places he seldom shared with me or, I hoped, any of his previous girlfriends.

A slow maroon bus drawing to a halt nearby offered me a plan. Even its driver seemed content – an Asian man, his mouth rounded into a circle, whistling to himself – it seemed. The bus was heading for the city centre. I climbed aboard. He was whistling 'Donald, Where's Your Troosers'. I bought an all-day ticket and transferred to a number 26 in the centre and headed down to the part of Edinburgh where he lived.

Lives.

At his flat, seeing his clothes lying around like flattened ghosts, the unwashed coffee mugs his lips recently tasted, the road-bike whose thousands of shared miles toned him, the Buddhas he collected, the simple spontaneous Zen paintings, imperfect circles he did in a single continuous brushstroke, I broke down and wept over this man who may or may not be dead or dying at this very moment. I needed to do something. I thought about hiding his road-bike so he could never cycle again, then I realised how crazy that was, but it was just the thought that his fixed-gear bike had looked every bit as good and solid and well-cared-for as that bike did, and now it was likely a mangled wreck. It probably didn't even look like a bike any more . . .

I cried again, cried, cried myself dry. When there were no tears left, to give myself something to do I cleaned his flat. That would please him if – *when* – he got home.

So I dusted everything, the Buddhas that were as usual the only dust-free things in the place, the famous desk, leaving the papers and laptop just as I found them. I swept and hoovered and mopped the vinyl wood flooring.

Afterwards I lay on his bed, offering silent prayers, inhaling the scent of him that rose from his pillow, his sheets. He had a pile of books, as per usual, stacked next to his beloved digital radio on the bedside table and I decided to take some of them with me when I went back to the hospital. I would also bring him some fruit and a change of clothes and what else would be good, a charger for his phone . . . he'd already have his iPod, which would have been in his bag and that should be at the hospital. I found his old backpack, and as I placed his belongings one by one into its blackness, its well-travelled blackness at that, I realised he would like that phrase and a greater thought hit my mind like lovely cool water; my actions – which speak louder than words (he wouldn't like that phrase, not because it wasn't true – it sometimes was – but because he wanted it not to be), yes, my actions proved I must have decided that he was alive, that he was going to live through this.

I caught myself whistling 'Donald, Where's Your Troosers' under my breath and smiled for the first time since it happened.

◡

I was pleased but not surprised that Nurse Stevenson was the first medical worker I encountered back at the hospital. I reckoned she was caring in a manner that almost transcended . . . well, normality. Not in any crazy *It's a Wonderful Life* way, but in a very real way. I'd always believed that good deeds bring their own rewards. I could still believe it true that decent people are always the happiest.

'How are you?' asked the nurse, rubbing my upper arm with her warm hand a couple of times.

'How am I?' For a moment, the question confused me. This wasn't about me. What did my wellness have to do with it? 'How's he doing?'

'He's been in the wars again. With himself. C'mon.'

Nurse Stevenson led me to a lift, our footsteps echoing in the sharp-smelling corridor. 'He's in a different room now. Things are looking better. You first.'

'Cheers. So you mean, like, see when he was fighting himself again – is that normal?'

The nurse pressed the 3 button, the lift doors closed and we began moving upwards though the lift was so slow you could hardly tell. 'One thing we realised is, he was allergic to the sheets in the last bed. Or maybe it was the washing powder. Anyway, we have him in a different kind of bedsheet now, and brand new, and a rash he had developed is going, plus he's not scratching at himself, which he had been doing. Now, sometimes trauma patients have a mechanism that kicks in that says "I know something is wrong, but I don't know what it is. I must have been in danger but I don't know if I'm still in danger" so they lash out. It's a self-protection thing. But with him –'

'Different, is he? Trust him.'

'It's not unheard of. It's like he's acting something out. Some people regularly do stuff like this just in their normal sleep. But with him –'

'Thing is, he's a very imaginative person and bringing characters to life is kind of what he does. Could that maybe have something to do with it?'

'Maybe. Maybe.'

'But?'

'But nothing. He's a one, all right. Oh, and we had words from him today.'

'I thought alive was enough – he's awake, too?' I was thrilled. For a second.

'No, no. We thought so at first, because he called out for a doctor. But it was Doctor *Jekyll* he was calling. And words like compassion. And cinnamon. And all these East Lothian place-names. And stabbing – which could have been a reference to pains he's having. We're medicating him to deal with that, so don't worry. We've been . . . Ah, here we are.' The lift doors opened and we stepped out. I followed Nurse Stevenson, memorising every word. 'Aye, we've been giving him some heavy-duty drugs, so it's fairly normal to hallucinate or have very vivid dreams. Like little films.'

I smiled. 'He does that anyway. He's a daydreamer. Oh, except when he's cycling. He cycles East Lothian a lot, that could be the place-names. He sees them all the time, they're printed on his brain.'

He lay in a new, but similar bed, and there were fewer machines feeding off him – or for him to keep alive, because you could say it was him who kept them going. More likely, it was both.

'I'll leave you two together then.'

'Thank you so much. You don't know what this means –'

'I know.' The nurse smiled and left, with a little bounce in her step. How could someone be so happy in a place of such sadness and death? Maybe because of all the ones they helped and saved. Knowing they were doing the helping and the saving. I regretted, not for the first time, that I hadn't studied Medicine at Edinburgh, as had been my original choice. How many people get offered a place at Edinburgh to do Medicine and then decide not to go to uni at all? I pushed my selfish thoughts down and sat on the bed beside my boyfriend. I took his hand and sandwiched it between my own, just as Nurse Stevenson had done. A serene smile came over his face.

And mine.

Then I grew aware there was something else in the room. It startled me, made me jump; I clutched at my chest, dropping his hand. I'd caught a shadowy movement out the corner of my eye. Now I looked, though, I marvelled at it – it was a butterfly, like a wee colourful bat flipflapping around the room. I read something once about souls leaving the body in the form of butterflies. Where did I read that? I couldn't remember, so I wasn't sure what I thought about it. I watched the butterfly flitting about the room. How could it be a soul? It moved about like something in a state of confusion, going round in circles, up around the light, over to the window, down to the bedside table, on to his mouth. Ha! I smiled at that, not that I was any less concerned about my boyfriend, but just – it landed on his mouth and flitted away and he spoke, as if the butterfly had touched a secret button on his mouth, he said, 'P-please,' then what sounded like, 'the last time.'

So I thought that was him telling me to get rid of the butterfly, and it occurred to me it wasn't hygienic to have it going about landing on people's mouths in a hospital so I opened a window and gave it its freedom. It wasn't a soul; it was a butterfly. Who knew, maybe a butterfly with a soul of its own.

He stopped talking for a while, though he fidgeted from time to time.

I decided to keep him calm by talking to him. I was heartened that he'd spoken, so I thought if I talked maybe he would respond or at least maybe he could hear me. I believed I could help him by talking, I needed to know I was helping.

I wasn't sure what to say. I'm a better listener than talker. I laughed at him when he encouraged me to try my hand at writing. Anyway, I began by telling him about cleaning his flat and bringing him all the things I'd brought, then I told him about how important it was that he kept doing as well as he was doing because I wanted him back and the sooner the better and oh yeah he'd had a wee crash but it wasn't too serious and everyone had looked after him well and he was almost fully recovered now and everything was going to be as cool as ever, cooler than ever, so the sooner he came back the better and . . . And I had a little cry but I kept it very very quiet so he wouldn't hear me in his secret place, wherever he was.

I told him about things we'd done together, about good things he had done in his life, about this and that and I talked on and on and on and . . . at some point I was shocked to discover I was running out of things to say. Talking without getting a response is a very hard thing to do. I got bored of the sound of my voice and was worried he would, too.

I wondered how he could get up in front of sometimes very large audiences and perform without just having a total breakdown and running off the stage in a mad frenzy of get-me-out-of-here like you sometimes experience in a bad dream. Whenever he did look nervous up there I told him afterwards he didn't look in the slightest bit nervous. It wasn't a lie, only a small white fib. A nun once told me that lying is sometimes forgivable. The example was if you're hiding Jews in your attic in 1940s Germany and some Nazis come to your door and ask if you are hiding any Jews you must lie and say no as that is the thing to do for the greater good. I worried about this, mind you, because life is rarely so clear-cut. It's not always easy to recognise the Nazis, is it?

I realised with a start I'd been babbling again so I had a wee brainwave and decided that I would read to him instead of talking gibberish at him. He was almost scared of silence at night, had to fall asleep with the radio on, or an audiobook, or calm instrumental music.

I picked up the book that was, for obvious reasons, the most important one to him before the accident: Robert Louis Stevenson's *The Strange Case of Dr Jekyll and Mr Hyde*. He owned half a dozen book versions and at least four film versions of this story. He was doing a play about it. Doing a play! The phrase was 'adapting it for the stage'. They had just finished casting when the accident happened. He loved the whole process of writing a play, then watching the characters come to life when actors took them in front of an audience. It was, he'd said, like watching something move from one person's mind to another, then seeing it come to life in a way that was predicted and unpredictable.

Sometimes when he sat there writing and he was really into it, he mouthed the words to himself, quietly at first, but after a while he would be reading them aloud, acting them out, oblivious to the fact I was lying there on the couch, smiling behind a newspaper.

One day, we were walking along Princes Street and we overheard a young girl yelling into her mobile phone, 'Oh, you changed your mind, did you? What did you do with the nappy?' and he laughed and said, 'That's like something Harris would say,' and I said, 'Who's Harris?' and his hand shot up to his mouth and he giggled and said, 'A character I invented,' and started laughing at himself. I love people who don't take themselves too seriously.

At a reading once someone put their hand up and asked about empathy, and he had stopped and frowned and stared at nothing for ages on the stage without even getting self-conscious and then at last he just said, 'To the writer, everyone wears a sign round their neck saying "Consider what it is like to be me".'

I'd never actually read the Jekyll and Hyde story, and wasn't sure I'd even seen a film version at any stage of my life. Maybe I would watch it with him when he came back to the land of the liv – when he was himself again. As with a lot of common stories, I reckoned I didn't really need to read the book or even see the film. It was just about a guy who's pure good and he drinks a potion that makes him pure evil and that bit of him takes over and in the end he can't be himself any more. Or, that evil was within him all the time but only now could he admit it. Or did the monster kill him in the end? Maybe he killed the monster?

Aye, maybe it was about killing the self.

That might tie in with the Buddhist stuff he was always banging on about; killing the self, 'extinction of the ego' was the phrase he trotted out. He was beginning to take all that stuff more seriously than ever when the crash happened. What kind of karma's that?

I opened the book, which was slim and had those beautiful old Victorian illustrations. Books are always more enjoyable to read when they look good. When and why did they decide to stop illustrating books so nicely? A sad smile came across my face at the thought of all these publishers having a meeting at which they decided from now on to make their books less attractive.

I began to read: 'Chapter One. Story of the door. Mister Utterson the lawyer was a man of rugged countenance, that was never lighted by a smile; cold, scanty and embarrassed in discourse; backward in sentiment; lean, long, dusty, dreary and yet somehow lovable.' The end part of that sentence made the rest of it worthwhile. The idea that someone as boring as that could be lovable was . . . well, lovely. Like, there's someone out there for everyone.

I continued, trying to keep my voice interesting, going up and down like a newsreader's, but more personal, warmer: 'At friendly meetings, and when the wine was to his taste, something eminently human beaconed from his eye; something indeed which never found its way into his talk, but which spoke not only in these silent symbols of the after-dinner face, but more often and loudly in the acts of his life.' Now that was a good way of putting it, 'when the wine was to his taste'. I remembered how my uncle would change after a drink. He became a different person altogether. First, his eyes would glow – 'beacon out' a writer might put it – with an unnatural light. Yes, the glaze on his eyes. And he would talk too loudly and say things that were over-opinionated. Controversial. Normally he had a smile for everyone. 'And fuck the lot of them, send them home. Fucking fuckers that they are.' His language made me blush to my fingertips. Oh, and the things he did – like, getting up to dance with the standard lamp or pretending his hand got stuck to the cat and he couldn't let go and the cat would get terrified and scratch him all to blazes and secretly I'd be cheering the cat. He'd keel over, fall asleep the second he hit the deck. My mum – his own sister – would put him to bed. Undress him and everything. Imagine. I shuddered. And the worst part was, the next day he wouldn't remember any of it, like something wiped his mind clean and life went on as normal until the next time he picked up a drink. I couldn't remember if he had lost his faith when he started drinking, or if he had started drinking because he'd lost his faith. Maybe he himself had forgotten.

But the thought now struck me. What if my boyfriend's mind was wiped clean like that? Wasn't that even quite a common thing in these circumstances? I should have studied Medicine, saved lives in a hospital, working alongside people like Nurse Stevenson. And what if he no longer loved me? What if he no longer even *remembered* me?

I thought again about where we go when we die.

I pictured myself at my uncle's funeral, standing at his open grave. I tossed a handful of dirt at his boxed corpse. Cold arrowy rain picked at my face. Inside I felt something that was not emptiness but was close to emptiness, just like how my face felt cold but not cold enough to be numb. A strange urge grew in me to yank my coat off and tear my blouse and bra away and let the cold and rain wash over my naked breasts, my torso, let it cleanse me to an icy nothingness. I wanted to be empty and pure and unfeeling.

I gazed at the wooden coffin that day and remembered a time me and my uncle sat in a café in Inverness. Why were we there? I couldn't for the life of me remember. But there we sat and my uncle looked at me for a long time, an uncomfortable time, with a curious glint in his eyes. Not curious because it was creepy, but curious because it wasn't. Maybe it was no more than the changing Highland light outside. And at last my uncle spoke and he said to me, 'When . . . when death comes, I hope . . .'

I hardened a little inside, embarrassed, and turned to the window, while my uncle swallowed his sentence – gulped it down for ever – and I wondered how many people would be at his funeral and whether he would die in pain and knowledge or pass away in the drifting blankness of sleep. Then my uncle stifled a half-sob and I just sat there watching the rain slide down the glass of the window, and my uncle breathed heavily like a man with a problem, which he was, and I sat and stared and ignored him until he too turned and watched the raindrops slide down the glass of the window.

Shortly after that I was alive and my uncle was dead and I was throwing dirt at his boxed corpse, an odd, but sometimes almost appropriate tribute the living pay to the dead, like the living can reach the dead.

I had to fight to keep from crying now.

Still, I had no time for self-pity. I brought a memory to mind that always cheered me up. It was a time my boyfriend and I visited a graveyard, a morbid hobby of his. In this graveyard in Morningside – that was a laugh in itself, you wouldn't expect Morningside residents to do anything as undignified as dying – anyway, in this graveyard we were both giggling inappropriately at life and, more so, death, it was almost as if we were drunk. Death can do that to you – make you come outside of yourself, like that crazy thinking that had come over me at my uncle's funeral.

Anyway, holding on to one another after a fit of laughter, we approached this one guy's headstone which read: 'He was a good man.'

I was appalled. I said, 'That's the best they could come up with? That's like "He was competent."'

And he started riffing on it. 'Yeah, he didn't fail *too* badly. He was average. He did the job without flair, without merit. But he didn't botch it. He very rarely fixed what wasn't broke.'

I joined in. 'And he only sometimes broke what was fixed.'

'"xactly . . . Jeez, talk about damning with faint praise. Praise that faint probably damned him somewhere south of Thatcher.' There was a pause and he put on a mischievous frown. 'Did they hate him? I mean, they should have just gone the whole way and put on his gravestone: "He was anatomically correct."'

I laughed hard at that. 'Emphasis on *was*.'

For days, weeks, months, afterwards, every time I heard that expression echoing through my mind – *He was anatomically correct* – I laughed out loud.

Oh, there was another bit. He'd also said in that dry way he sometimes had, 'That's what I want on my gravestone: *He was anatomically correct. RIP. LOL.*'

I didn't want to think about that, not at all. So I carried on reading this story that had such an unusual structure and was stranger and slower and less eventful and deeper than I had expected. I wondered what the author was like. He came from Edinburgh, I knew that. Studied law, was it, or just hung around pubs with prostitutes? I'd seen part of a documentary about him once, Robert Louis Stevenson. He died young, I definitely thought I remembered that. After I'd finished the book, I would read the introduction; that might tell me about his life.

And that's what I did. I read books to him, I was tactile with him – holding his hand or blowing on his forehead or even kissing him, right on the lips, sometimes. Well, you never knew – that's what happened in fairytales and besides why couldn't physical contact like that help?

I read the Buddhist books and learned a lot about what things really are as opposed to what they seem. Some of it was hard to understand, but the big questions in life aren't supposed to be easy, are they?

I learned some interesting things, too, ones I didn't expect to, while he was in his – sleep, we'll call it a sleep. That's what it was – a very deep sleep. No – 'resting', like actors do. He'd like that one. While he was resting.

O

Not long before he woke he used the expression 'an absolute Bodhisattva of a woman'; these, I swear, are the words he used. I recognised them for two clear and different reasons. One is that when we first met, in that lovely golden springtime of our relationship, and which wasn't when I thought about it that long ago – a year just – we had gone out for a meal down in Leith.

He had at first seemed a little unsure about the idea but was too polite to say so. I pushed him to tell me why he looked reluctant. Okay, I even said something along the lines of 'Don't you want to see me tonight?' when I already knew that he did; maybe that was playing games with him a little. Anyway, he told me that the place I'd suggested – an Italian restaurant with a sea view – might not be good because you have to be wary of dining in places that have great views; it's often the view that attracts customers, not the food. The chefs can afford to be a little lazy. He had once worked in a restaurant that didn't have a good view.

'Well,' I told him, a little hurt – most of it pretend hurt, to be honest – 'I chose it thinking of you, because of the sea view and because it's Italian.'

And he relented, and as it happened we had a beautiful meal and for some reason the waitress even gave him free ice-cream along with his tiramisu, and over coffee he had just looked at me and held my gaze for a few moments, not in an uncomfortable way like it would be with most people, just the opposite. He looked into my eyes and said, and his voice was quiet as usual, but it broke a little with emotion and he told me, 'I just had a vision of you – your face changed in front of my eyes and you looked for just a second like a Buddha-to-be, all serene and kind. Compassionate. You are an absolute Bodhisattva of a woman.'

Now, I hadn't been too sure what he meant. Did he really see my face change like that? What did the words mean? But it was that lovely early time in a relationship when everything is at its best, everything feels special; that whole period you just wish could last for ever. And I didn't want to come across as stupid. I wasn't thick, far from it, and I made him laugh and in all truth it took a pretty damn clever sense of humour to do that. I didn't want to spoil the moment by asking what he meant. His imagination was a bit, well, overactive, you might say.

And now, those words had come from his mouth again. 'An absolute Bodhisattva of a woman.' My feelings were mixed, though, as I had read those very words to him in a short story just the day before. Was he remembering that? Or was he remembering me? At least I learned from one of the non-fiction books what a Bodhisattva is – an enlightened person who has deferred Buddhahood because they have resolved to help others achieve enlightenment first.

Quite a compliment, then! But I didn't know the first thing about enlightenment. I lived a simple life and tried to put others before myself and hoped I did the right thing and that was it. I got on with things by being myself; I didn't analyse or meditate or anything like that. I was spontaneous, and if a bus happened to turn up and suggest itself to me, I jumped on it. So my life had a spirit of adventure about it, unlike his. Or, rather, his life was full of adventure but he never saw it that way. He was an observer more than a participant. Maybe cycling was good for him because it made him both.

Would he be able to cycle again? Would he want to? I hoped he wouldn't want to, but it would have to be his choice. I just hoped he'd come back able to make choices like that. There were so many questions in my mind and it was hard, at times, not to voice them out loud, to shout them at him. I even wanted, once or twice, to slap his face hard to see if it would make him wake up. I had to leave the room a number of times because I could no longer fight back the tears. I would sob in the bathroom stalls, using that horrible rough tissue paper to dab my eyes.

Again, reading helped. It made me feel like I was helping and it kept my mind occupied. Occupied, it has to be said, with good things. Maybe reading the Jekyll and Hyde story would help him unconsciously or subliminally with writing the play. Why not? After all, there must be something to that; it was how advertising worked, wasn't it? A probably billion-pound industry. And the Buddhisty books gave me a feeling of comfort and even serenity. Good word. I'm going to use it more. An even better one was equanimity, but you can't slip that one into a conversation.

I read and read and read. When my voice started getting sore I made myself tea. When she was on duty, Nurse Stevenson made me tea. It was her own tea, that she brought in herself, cinnamon tea. She said it had calming properties and would help me better than normal tea; you'd be surprised how much caffeine there is in normal tea. But cinnamon calms you and besides it tastes great. True.

So, I took to drinking cinnamon tea and I felt I was somehow – and the man would understand this – drinking the lovely calm essence of Nurse Stevenson herself. Come to think of it, *she* if anyone was an absolute Bodhisattva of a woman.

Writing helped. I had never really written about myself before, never kept a diary for more than a few days. He wrote in the 'I' – it's the first person, isn't it? – almost all the time, whether he was talking about himself or, as was more often the case, inventing characters and situations. There was probably a term for it. Maybe you could call it *method writing*. Where had I heard that expression? Anyway, I liked it; it applied to him.

That said, his mind was not always a good place for him to go. I wished I could change that about him. Imagine carrying about inside you, like a disease, something that is bad for you. I had no doubts he spent too much time inside his own mind. Sometimes his mind was kind to him. I could coax the good mind to the surface, and so could cycling and so could meditation. Oh, and of course writing. I was really coming to understand this.

So I wrote about him and myself, and writing the words gave me comfort just as reading the words gave him comfort. The writing, I did at home – his home, in fact; I made it a little tradition that I would keep his flat neat and tidy until he was ready to get back to living there himself. I liked sleeping in his bed, though sleep didn't come easily. I would sit up in bed with a pen and paper and just write, write, write. I was surprised how easily the words came. I'd read a book to him by a guy whose name I couldn't pronounce and on the first page it had talked about how interconnected everything is and proved it by describing how that page came together. Amazing. You could think the same about the very page I held in my hands right there and then.

And I felt that by writing at all, I was connecting with him on some level, or at least trying to. I was proving my need to connect with him since he was himself a writer. I wouldn't tell him that it felt easier than he always made out. No, I *would*, once he was better. We could make it a running joke.

Well, that's about it for now. It's morning and I had a dream last night that you woke up today and I have a feeling it will come true. I put faith in dreams, as you know, and even the weird ones, the surreal ones, have a truth if we can only learn to decipher them. That's what I believe, anyway. And you are going to be surprised – chuffed, even – that I wrote all this.

(And remind me to ask you if it is Robert *Loo*-iss or Robert *Loo*-ee Stevenson and what's the proper way to say Jekyll? Hope I said them right.)

So, this is my last piece of writing to you, my darling, but maybe it's the start of my writing career, ha ha. I'm going to come and see you today and you're going to wake up, Mac, and I'm going to give you a great massive hug for a long long time and even though our eyes will be closed we'll know in that big warm hug that we're both smiling as one.

Love, love
Julie

xx

Someone with cool cinnamon-scented breath was blowing on my forehead.

'*Nnnnguh?*' I said. I opened my eyes, slow, unsure, not frightened. Hands thrust my glasses on my face, clipping my ears painfully.

A young woman's forehead. Behind, above, it a pure white ceiling. They should put a 'Welcome Back' sign there, or a TV or a picture of God.

Such wide blue eyes she had, eyes that gasped.

'Oh God,' she said. 'You're back. I knew it!'

In those lovely eyes of hers, tears melted into being, and she leaned that inch or so closer and kissed my forehead where she'd just been blowing on it; a few tears dripped and landed on my head with a warm sensual spatter. 'Oh, sorry, sorry.' She wiped my forehead with her hand, tender, and sat back on the bed gaping at me in an ecstasy of disbelief. She rested a hand on my arm, which was under the blanket. My other hand lay inert on the bed with a drip attached. I yearned for a more direct touch, her skin on mine. At the same time, I didn't feel like moving was much of an option. My body felt heavy. Heavytired.

How glossy her long hair was, framing that face of wide-eyed sadness and contemplative innocence. Her face was shadowless, bright like a flower. 'You're wondering where you are, yes?'

'Why – why – blowing?'

'Why was I blowing on your forehead?' She laughed as she wiped her aftertears away. 'Trust you. Never mind the big questions, the fact you actually di–' Her face grew serious then relaxed. 'I was blowing on your forehead because I read somewhere it comforts people, makes them feel good. There were times you – well, you were kind of frantic, kicking and pushing and, like, um, *fighting yourself* in the bed. Wow, they had to keep injecting you with the good stuff.'

My memory was hazy as a long-buried mirror.

I remembered a dim thing called time. I couldn't figure how it worked or how it connected to me.

'I *knew* you'd make it back. I even had a dream last night that today would be the day, if you can believe that. Like a premonition. I've gotta call the nurses and let them know you're back with us.'

'Where have I been?'

'You're in hospital, yeah? But it's all going to be okay. You remember me, don't you? Please say you do. You can't forget me.'

'Juliette.'

She tittered. 'If that's how you want to say it. Close enough, sweetie. Don't you worry about anything. You haven't exactly been yourself. But. It's all good. It's all good.'

She reached above my head and pressed a button that sent an alarm ringing through the pure white room and whatever lay beyond it.

○

A nurse bustled into the room and moved towards my bed as though she were on tiptoe. Her lips presented a rueful smile, happy and smart at once. 'Welcome back. We've been waiting for you. How d'you feel?'

'Uh. Am I alive?'

Juliette gave a little snigger of joy.

The nurse's smile grew wider. She had a wise smile. 'You'd be surprised how many people ask that. And very lucky you are, too. Most people only get one chance at life. Now, do you remember your name?'

'You're . . . Yours is Nurse Stevenson.'

Juliette blanched, flicked her head towards me then the nurse then back to me. 'How d'you know that?'

'Says so on my uniform.'

I closed my eyes for a moment, brought a hand up to my forehead. My mind had no past, no future, no sure memories. That wasn't quite right. I had memories, lots of them. The more I thought of them, the more of them there were.

'The doctor will be round shortly to examine you properly. Meanwhile –' Nurse Stevenson gazed at the machinery above me. 'Your signs are good.' She picked up a clipboard from the end of my bed. 'All things considered . . . Oh, and that's quite a girlfriend you have there.' Nurse Stevenson pointed to Juliette, who was sniffling back fresh tears. 'She came to see you and read to you every day and every evening. And,' she swapped a look, a private joke, with Juliette, 'she blew on your forehead to soothe your mind.'

Juliette's sniffs turned to half-giggles. 'That's what brought him round, me blowing his mind. Tell her!'

I smiled. 'It's true.'

'Now. Are you in any pain?' asked the nurse.

I thought about this. 'No, I don't think so. Not pain, just twinges. All over. Like two out of ten pain, nothing to bother about. But I – I've got a lot of questions I–'

'Rest up first. We need to get you examined now you're conscious again. The doctor's on his way. You might feel more pain as the drugs wear off. We've been monitoring your progress, and it was quite the task finding the optimal pattern for your pain relief. At times you were very . . . animated while you were unconscious.'

'You sure were. Well, look, I guess I know the drill now. I better slink off if the doctor's going to be here,' said Juliette, getting to her feet and leaning in towards me. 'I'll be back in no time, I promise.' She kissed me soft and slow on the forehead and stroked a gentle hand along my cheek. She gave me a wonderful look, then turned and with a twinkle breezed out of the room.

Nurse Stevenson patted her on the shoulder on the way out, then she and I faced each other in a curious, almost familiar silence.

Nurse Stevenson recovered first. 'You were so animated. Must be one heck of an inner life you lead.'

Though her manner was comforting it was also a little strange. 'It was hell, mostly. I feel like I know you. Have we met before?' I asked.

'No. Only when they brought you in – and you were unconscious then.'

'Really?'

'Very. When else would we meet?'

'And, um, I hope you don't mind me asking. But, was I – was I dead?'

'Enough questions. You have to take things easy. It's like this. You're not just the owner of your body. You're its manager.'

'I seem to have this memory. I mean, there's lots of them, but this one just came at me, like a flashback. I'm having loads and loads of them. They're non-stop. But it's an old film and I saw it *ages* ago . . . W C Fields – is that his name?'

'I've heard of him.'

'Yeah, so he goes into a bank, with his big red nose, glassy eyes and all, not that I'm one to talk given how I must look right now – anyway, W C Fields goes into a bank and the bank teller or clerk or whatever they're called, she says to him because he wants to withdraw a lot of money, "Can you identify yourself?" and he, he asks for a mirror, she hands over her compact and he looks into it and goes, "Yep, that's me."'

Nurse Stevenson gave an indulgent little laugh. 'I think I've heard that one, it's not bad. Is that what you were dreaming about then?'

'No, in fact, sorry, but I really need to talk abou–'

'Enough for now. Rest a little for me, okay.'

'I feel like an astronaut who went to the moon to write a letter home.'

'The doctor will be here soon.'

'How long?'

'If you want, close your eyes and he'll be here.'

'I'm lucky to be alive, amn't I?'

Nurse Stevenson's mouth straightened and she thought for a moment or two before replying, 'Honestly?' She paused again. 'At times it seemed all it would take to send you one way or the other was a breath, or a thought.'

I let my limbs melt into the bed. I closed my eyes, but I didn't expect to sleep as part of me felt sure I'd been asleep for a long time. Nevertheless I sank into the bed in the darkness of my shut eyes and the mattress upheld me as I sank into it, deeper and deeper, and soon I was asleep with only an image of Juliette's face in my mind, changed, softer and more beautiful than I'd remembered it. Like the girl I always wanted. Gorgeous and kind and thoughtful and intelligent. Her face hovered before mine for a long time.

Behind her face, between it and the ceiling, a ragged succession of pictures floated. Ideas. Memories. I had the feeling of being nested, of everything being nested inside something bigger. Images, stories, identities.

I knew, and didn't, that I was asleep.

The doctors took a long time examining me. I was an interesting case, not a person; they tended to fob off or disregard my questions. I let them get on with it. They had, after all, saved my life. They didn't owe me anything more. I think I even fell asleep again while the doctors were still there.

At last Juliette returned, in a yellow summer dress, bright and lovely as sunshine.

I marvelled. 'You came here every visiting hour?'

Juliette closed her eyes and nodded, parodying a proud child.

'And you sat on that horrible plastic seat?'

'Or on the bed beside you, though I wasn't meant to in case I popped any of your cables out. Nurse Stevenson was dead nice. I've never met anyone so kind. She spoke to the other staff and they let me stay as long as I wanted, so I came every day and stayed as long as I could.'

'Why?'

'Because you were . . . in a bad way. I'll tell you later everything that happened. I was scared.'

I sucked air in through my teeth. 'Scared. Man. I don't know if I even wanna *think* about scared yet. What did you even *do* all the time you were here? Must've been boring.'

'At first I spoke to you. Just talked. About this and that. Then I ran out of things to talk about. Hard to believe, I know. It's really tough making stuff up all the time – course, you'd know about that. So, what I did, I had a brainwave and took a pile of books from your bedside table, no, not that one, dummy, your own one from home. I have your spare key, remember.' She paused. 'Well, I guess why would you. We'll need to work on your memory. Anyway, I let myself in, cleaned your flat up a bit, did your dishes in that stupid small sink, and took all these books in and read them to you. That was good thinking, the books. And other times, just stroked your arms, held your hand, blew on your forehead 'cause I was told these things can help.' She hesitated, then grinned and blushed. 'Kissed you once or twice. Sorry.'

'Sorry for what?'

'It's probably sexual harassment, isn't it? Kissing someone in a coma. Bit your lip once, too.'

We both laughed a little.

Something occurred to me. 'My flat.'

'Yeah?'

'What size is my kitchen sink?'

'*Tiny.*'

'Is it shrinking?'

She went Glaswegian to lighten the moment. 'Gonnae no keep taking that morphine, pal?'

'Its not shrinking, is it?'

'That's a real question?'

I nodded, solemness in my eyes.

'Your sink, my dear, is the same size it always was. A bit too small, to be truthful, but no smaller than ever.'

'What books did you read me?'

'Oh, different ones. D'you think you could hear? They say hearing is the last sense to go and the first to come back. That's what Nurse Stevenson said.'

'I don't know for sure.'

'Well, I read *The Strange Case of Dr Jekyll and Mr Hyde*, obviously, since you were working on that one when the crash . . . Shit, they asked me not to mention that to you yet.'

'Juliette! You've got to tell me.'

She tittered. 'That's funny.'

'The hell's funny? I wanna know about my crash.'

195

'How you say my name. Well, I heard of one guy on the internet who came out of a coma and he spoke only Flemish. He forgot he ever knew English. So I guess it's all relative.'

'Was the accident my fault? I don't remember it – I was just cycling along, there was mist –'

'I don't think there was mist that day. Maybe. The cops'll want to chat with you, but to be honest I don't think they know much. It's not on CCTV and they have no witnesses, just the aftermath – aftermath, horrible word.'

'What else were you reading to me?'

'You had a ton of Buddhist books. I actually found them interesting. So I read quite a few of them. There was this one, I'm going to get a tattoo of it.'

'A book?'

'A *quote* from one of the books. "If you speak or act with a calm, bright heart, then happiness follows you, like a shadow that never leaves."'

I gave a dry laugh. 'That hardly describes me – or you.'

'Hey!' Her eyes flared in mock outrage. 'Does *so* describe me. I'm your happy shadow.'

I hesitated. Juliette was not at all how I remembered her. She was . . . nicer. Way nicer.

'No, uh, no – sorry. I don't know why I said that. I'm not, not quite myself. Where you going to get it?'

'Same place you got yours.'

'In Glasgow?'

She laughed and punched me delicately. 'On the arm!'

'Where's my tattoo that says "Lift your bike out into the open day. Ride forth"?'

'Um . . . you don't have one. Unless the doctors tattooed you while you were out of it and I'm pretty sure that's against NHS rules. Talking of tattoos, I keep meaning to ask before you go off on tangents, how's the pain now?'

I frowned, thought about it. 'I guess not bad, since I had to think about it. Well, there's pain, yeah, but not *pain* pain, if you know what I mean.'

'They've totally brought down the amount of drugs you were on. At one point, you were like – wow.'

'What?'

'Just – out of it. I mean –' she glanced at the door and when she looked round again I was shocked to see tears forming in her eyes. 'You – you . . .' She buried her head in her hands and bent forwards in the plastic seat.

'I – what . . .?' I wanted to comfort her, but a panic rose in my chest. A machine above me started beeping.

'No, no, it's nothing,' she said and looked at me with an unconvincing smile. 'The important thing is you're here.'

'I'm alive.' I nodded. 'I am, amn't I?'

Her smile grew to authentic, which appeased me – and the machine, which stopped beeping.

'Tell me straight, though,' I said, 'I died, didn't I?'

'You'll need to talk to the doctors about that. I mean, I think you came close . . .'

'Did I have a heart attack? I had a feeling . . . a knife in the heart. Someone knifed me in the heart.'

'No, no – not a heart attack. And no one knifed you in the heart.' She gave an involuntary laugh that somehow lifted my mood. I liked how she was treating me like a person, not a casualty. 'What are you like? There was kick-ass concussion, Niagara-like blood loss, they had you on major drugs . . . What else, um . . . You had some, like, all these wounds and stuff. You must have an *atlas* of bruises on you. Oh – there was some metal – a part of your bike – a

197

spoke – broke loose and stuck into your chest. But thankfully it got stuck in the muscle.'

'The heart is a muscle.'

'It wasn't your heart. It was your chest, your pectoral muscle. It didn't go too deep.'

'It would still have hurt, though, yeah?'

'I imagine so.'

'I had this crazy idea that when I was in Italy –'

'Which time?'

'I've only been once.'

'You told me you've been three times.'

'When?'

'Before all this.'

'No, when was I there last?'

'Like, I don't know, years. A few years ago.'

'Wow. Just – wow.' I shook my head. 'I had this supervivid dream that a pros– an Italian woman came into my room and stuck a knife in her own heart.'

'Well, that's not mental at all,' she said with a grin. 'Still, that's my artistic genius.' Her face changed. She sighed. 'Manoman, it is so good to have you back.'

'Yeah, and then later – I think I was going to stick a knife in your heart –'

Her eyes widened and at almost the same time she started laughing. 'Oh yeah? Stick a knife in my heart, would you, after all I've done for you? There's gratitude.'

'Well, it was all over that Woolfe thing.'

'Uh –'

'The play! Oh my God, how's the play? What's happening?'

'Well, obviously they postponed rehearsals till you're on the mend.'

'You. Are. Joking.'

'No.'

'They did that for me?'

'Well, of *course* they did, what else were they going to do?'

'What about Woolfe?'

'Wolf is fine. Arrogant as ever, but, as you said, the perfect guy for the role. Roles. Like you also said, the arrogance is just a mask for insecurity. Sweetie, get some rest. You might not think so, but you need it. I'll be back later.'

'And Cassandra?'

Juliette's face hardened. 'Your ex? You do know she's your ex? Like, very ex? From, I dunno, three years ago. She wasn't exactly nice to you. We don't talk about her. She smelled and never washed.'

'But she did exist?'

'Aye, unfortunately. Anyway, they only let me in if I promised I'd be no more than twenty minutes. I better let you rest up. Things are going to take a while. I think I heard they're going to unhook you from some of this machinery, make you less of a cyborg.'

'I want to get up and go outside.'

'Patience, my dear.'

She got up from her chair, leaned in and kissed me on the forehead, two brief cinnamon-scented kisses, and then a slower third.

'I love you,' she whispered.

Love me? I considered what I'd been through. I? Who was I?

We do things. Sometimes consciously, other times unconsciously. We fight existential emptiness either head-on or by ignoring it. We use memory and imagination; we reify our lives, our sense of being, our *selves*. We hold on to memories and create and re-create our self-image, our narrative, our autobiography. In thought and action we are in a constant fight to preserve a sense of self. Egotism.

We are, as long as we have this life, committing continual acts of self-preservation and self-creation. The solid core of self is not a fixed entity, it is an illusion.

What continually reinforces the illusion is its functionality.

What is happening at this very moment?

What is *this*?

My eyes opened.

I reached out an automatic hand for my glasses.

Julie. Gazing at me with a vivid pink smile.

I thought back to my experiences, How come dreams are in full-focus?

My heart panged.

Julie was not in reality like Juliette.

I couldn't believe Julie's devotion.

A lot of things bothered me. I was returning to normal in some ways – feeding myself, going to the toilet on my own – but I was still not my old self. Some things I found hard to let go.

My memory was coming back, editing, sifting fact from fiction. Julie and I had fought, argued. There were times she hated me. Times I hated her. No, times I hated myself. Look how thoughtful and compassionate she was to me, despite everything. I didn't deserve this kindness.

'Jekyll and Hyde,' I said, 'which one am I being now?'

'I don't get you.'

'Which one?'

There was a long pause.

'You're being you. More or less.'

'Aye, which though? *More?* Or *less?*'

'Man, I don't know whether to ask them to put you back on more drugs or let them all wear off. You're a little confused, is all. Totally natural. I read something to you, I think it was talking about meditation, and it said "the non-doing in which nothing is left undone". That one helped me a lot. I thought of you meditating, like meditating deeply when you were . . . resting.'

'Ha.'

'No, but you moved and jerked around a lot at times, flailing out, like, you reminded me of a kid playing swingball against himself, and at the end, when they had to give you a massive sedative 'cause you had actually started hitting yourself badly, you chilled out and then just, just looked so peaceful. When I noticed that, that's the night I went home and dreamt you came back. Non-doing. I just loved the sound of that. Non-doing. Just sounds so effortless. And I guess when nothing was left undone, you came back to us.'

'Journey? Hitting myself? Yeah, that sounds like . . . I can sort of remember.'

'I dunno what journey though. Your path to . . . a new you? Does that sound horribly holistically chakratastic?'

'Listen, was I a total pain before the accident? Am I – was I – a bad person? Be honest.'

'No! No. I mean, you were a bit, y'know . . . unpredictable at times. Contradictory. But we're all like that. There's no such thing as an all-good person.'

'Mmm. I wonder.'

She laughed. 'Well, if there is, it's not you.'

I must've looked hurt. She added, 'Nor me. Nor anyone. We can all be judgemental, or just – plain bad. There were times,

201

especially reasonably early on in our relationship, when you said things that hurt me. But I was just getting to know you, and, and it turned out you weren't this idealised person I wanted you to be. Guess what, the same goes for how you probably thought of me. Because you *definitely* idealise people.'

'I can't remember, but I think I thought we split up.'

'Well, we didn't. But what it was, was – your mood swings were bigger and faster than other people's. Like, your whole personality changed. You were never physically abusive – you *do* know you would never be capable of that – but you could be controlling, possessive. And when you were unhappy, which I'm sorry but I have to say was often, you kind of projected the blame on to me. And you'd be nice to all the people you met through work, but then when you were with me, you'd be, like, back to morose. Total Jekyll and Hyde, which is the funny thing. And all these people would come up to me at your events, and they'd be like, "Oh God, you're so lucky to be going out with him, he's just so sweet and funny. Why do I never meet guys like that?" And I'd be, like, thinking, *He's not like that at all. He's a fake.*'

That word wounded me. I wished I could cry. I buried my face in my hands. 'God, I'm sorry. I'm so sorry. You deserve better.'

'Not *fake* fake. Just . . . We're all like that, to some extent. And because of your career, it was as though you were being encouraged to actually *develop* this fake self. I mean, you see it in the media all the time – this, like, narcissistic self instead of the real you, which was warm and caring and insecure even. You had – not even *low* self-esteem, but *no* self-esteem. But what happened was you nurtured the wrong self, the overcompensating one, and everyone else helped you along, because they never saw the real you, they saw the overdone one-sided you they wanted to see.'

'That's the way with actors. Writers. I mean. I'm so sorry –'

She frowned. 'Yes, I guess that is the way with actors. But you're not an actor. You're a writer. Better yet, you're a person. 3D. Real-life.'

'I can't tell you how sorry I am.'

'No, no. Because the thing is, I realised when, when we almost lost you, I love you. I love you despite all that. It just means you're human.'

'I don't want to be "just" human.' I heaved a sigh. 'And d'you think dreams are a punishment? Or an exorcism? D'you think we have power over them, or that they have some sway over us?'

'I think you think too much, is what I think.'

'You're right. Who can separate dream and dreamer?'

She laughed. 'Aye, that's exactly what I said.'

'And, like – what is love?'

'Another strange question – how many's that in a row? Don't you *love me*?' She reached out, her arms stretched wide, her fore-head wrinkled, an expectant look on her face.

Yield to warmth, always.

We hugged. I did love her. Did I? If I couldn't be sure of who I was, then I couldn't be sure of who she was. I kept thinking, if love is a desire to *possess* a person, it's not love. 'I do. I love you.' *Just not in that way.*

○

I sat up in my bed with my netbook lying closed on my lap in front of me. I couldn't quite bring myself to open it and its docu-ments yet so I just stared at it in an empty stupor.

I looked up and realised I was sitting in the heart of a perfect silence. Everything was settled deep into stillness. I looked out the window and in the sky opposite a full moon shone. It was the same moon at which I had marvelled so many times in my life, in so many different places. And yet it wasn't the same; this moon was unique. For that matter, I wasn't the same person. I was a little better than I feared, a little better than my fears. But not at all as decent a person as I would like to be.

The serene glow of the moon beautified the night sky.

I opened the netbook and as I did a pang of doubt flashed in my mind and I remembered being in a delightful fusty old bookshop one time – couldn't remember where for the moment – but I had that slight plummeting of the heart, like the heart itself just got punctured, when I noticed they were selling one of my own books. Second-hand. Someone didn't like my work. In my mind, this was physical evidence I was a failure even though I know the book everyone likes has never been written and never will be. We don't all like the same food, it would be a bland world we lived in if everyone liked the same books. So I bought my own book, second-hand, and as I walked along the street afterwards thinking about the directions the book's own life had taken, I heard peals of derisive laughter behind me, and when I turned round there was no one there.

The moonlight washed in through the window and meanwhile in this very hospital people I had never met were suffering and dying and surviving and thriving and changing under the compassionate hands of people who make it their business to sustain and improve life. Now light footsteps padded down the corridor, carrying a person with her own body and mind and health status and her own history of breathtaking moons and her own loves and doubts and memories, her own narratives. The more I thought of how unique and connected and vulnerable we are, all of us, on this tiny planet, the more my heart seemed to fill and then overflow with a soothing confidence.

Maybe we're like the moon, endlessly reflected, but ulti-mately one.

I placed my thumb on the little slider at the front of the netbook, and as I felt its plastic texture I slid it over to the right and the screen began to come to life with a brief trilling melody.

The wee white netbook took a few moments to gather its thoughts, readying itself. I did the same. The hospital was very quiet again. Its antiseptic smell comforted me; that pure simple clean scent reminded me of a blank piece of paper. Even the smooth bedsheets felt like a little blessing, stretched reassur-ingly tight against my legs. A rectangle of warmth silently hummed on my thighs under the netbook.

I thought of all that I had been through, how convinced I had been it was true while it happened. Had it happened? It had and it hadn't. Maybe dreams are like art, which Picasso said consisted of lies that tell a greater truth. There might not be people who believed the story, but there would be people who understood and appreciated the truth that made the lie. The truth that created the lie that told the greater truth.

I decided that I would ignore the play for the moment and start a fresh piece of writing. Instead of trying to control the mind, I would listen to it, let it offer its own lessons. I let the memories run through my mind like a film. I followed my mind's every projection. I let the mind test me, push me into dark places.

I began to discern, beneath the old swirl and drift of desire and suffering and loss and egotism, a deeper richer pattern of connections.

When freed from the craving, hatred and delusion that prevent one's self from being oneself, man is not truly two, but one.

I noticed the moon was reflected in the upper right-hand corner of my netbook's screen. I smiled. It was faint, but if you looked you could see it clearly enough. I looked round at the real thing and grinned. It was so large, suspended there stunningly bright in the wide sky.

I lifted my hands, paused, placed my fingertips on the keyboard. I began pushing on the keys in a pattern shaped by the circumstances my mind had brought about.

I tapped away at the keys, making a strange music in this place of living and dying, under the brilliance of the moon. After a while, the entire process was instinctive; I made no more effort to think about it than the moon did to shine. The words fell natural as light and I sat there on my bed tip-tap-tip-tapping the keys like playing a piano and the writing carried me along, as if I were being led towards something; yes, the writing flowed through me in a swift subtle contemplation and my physical body seemed to change. My skin didn't feel like a boundary but a connecting tissue, another part of this universe. Everything flowed, everything was part of an endless flow, as if one essence made and moves us all, and this, I realised, is the life that is; there isn't another reality that would be a better chance for me to be than this one. This is what there is.

I stayed awake all night typing. From time to time I would turn with a grin to stare at the huge moon hanging in mid-air outside there, a few hundred thousand miles away. I had never been so awake.

Curtain Call

Smattering of applause while some people cough and roll their eyes: the guy whose vehicle ate my bike.

Deep bow of respect and gratitude: Judy Moir, Neville Moir, Hugh Andrew, Sarah Morrison, Alison Rae, Jim Hutcheson, Jan Rutherford, Vikki Reilly, Anna Renz, Don Coutts and the Danube bike-ride documentary crew, Hi-Arts, the Scottish Arts Council, the Oppenheim-John Downes Trust, the Royal Literary Fund for the J B Priestley Award, my wonderful colleagues on the University of Edinburgh Creative Writing MSc 2009–2010 (Robert Alan Jamieson, Rajorshi Chakraborti, Lesley Glaister, Jane McKie, Alan Gillis) and all our students.

Standing ovation: Mum and Dad, Francis John MacNeil, Donald Mackay, Lynsey MacLeod, Elin Peterson, Lucinda Papezova, Lynda Flossy MacDonald, Willie Campbell, Ishbel Maria McFarlane and the many other inspiring friends who have blessed my life with their (almost) unfailing companionship, eccentricity and . . . wit. (Their wit sometimes failed).

I love you all, though I never seem able to tell you.
Well, I mean, I'm telling you now.
I love you.
For Mum and Dad

x

A Note on the Author

Kevin MacNeil was born and raised on the Isle of Lewis. A poet, novelist, aphorist, lyricist, screenwriter and playwright, his books include *Love and Zen in the Outer Hebrides, Be Wise Be Otherwise, The Callanish Stoned* and *The Stornoway Way*. His first book won the Tivoli Europa Giovani International Poetry Prize for best poetry collection published in Europe by a writer under 35. MacNeil was the inaugural Iain Crichton Smith Bilingual Writing Fellow and has held further prestigious writing residencies in Sweden (Uppsala University), Bavaria (Villa Concordia) and a number of other places, including lecturing on the Creative Writing MSc at Edinburgh University.

He often collaborates with visual artists and musicians. The William Campbell/Kevin MacNeil single 'Local Man Ruins Everything' was Single of the Week in *The Guardian,* in *The List* and on Steve Lamacq's radio show.

In 2009 he cycled 1,300km of the Danube, from the source to Budapest, on a single-speed fixed-gear track bike, for two cancer charities; the BBC filmed a documentary about his bike ride which took just a dozen cycling days.

www.kevinmacneil.com